Choice Summer

by Shirley Brinkerhoff

PUBLISHING
Colorado Springs, Colorado

CHOICE SUMMER
Copyright © 1996 by Shirley Brinkerhoff.
All rights reserved. International copyright secured.

Library of Congress Cataloging-in-Publication Data

Brinkerhoff, Shirley
    Choice summer / Shirley Brinkerhoff
        p. cm. — (The Nikki Sheridan series ; 1)
    Summary: After learning that she is pregnant, sixteen-year-old Nikki faces
the toughest decision of her life—whether to give birth to the baby or have an
abortion.
    ISBN 1-56179-484-8
    [1. Pregnancy—Fiction. 2. Abortion—Fiction. 3. Decision making—Fiction.
4. Christian life—Fiction.] I. Title. II. Series: Brinkerhoff, Shirley. Nikki Sheridan
series ; 1.
PZ7.B780115Ch   1996
[Fic]—dc20   96-5783
                                                                              CIP
                                                                              AC

Published by Focus on the Family Publishing,
Colorado Springs, CO 80995.
Distributed in the U.S.A. and Canada by Word Books, Dallas, Texas.

Cover design: Candi L. Park
Cover illustration: Cheri Bladholm

Printed in the United States of America
96 97 98 99 00/10 9 8 7 6 5 4 3 2 1

For Mark,
unfailing encourager, best of friends, love of my life.

And for Marcus, Melanie, and Ryan,
who taught me the indescribable value of each human life.

❧ One ❧

THE EXAMINING ROOM DOOR OPENED with a metallic click, and Nikki froze, her hands behind her neck. Her dark, curly hair swung down across her shoulders, free from the heavy, gold barrette she had been struggling to close around it.

She knew before the nurse said a word what the verdict would be.

"Sure enough, honey, you're pregnant!"

The barrette clattered against the tile floor. The nurse crossed the room and held out a round plastic disc for Nikki's inspection.

"See that little plus sign?" She leaned close, and Nikki pulled back slightly, away from the odor of sweaty hair. "If you're pregnant, you get a plus—if not, you get a little line, like a minus sign. Yours came up plus right away. How far along do you figure you are?"

Nikki's hands gripped the cold metal edge of the examining table, and she shifted her weight on the crackling white paper. The nurse raised her eyebrows in question, but Nikki

1

couldn't seem to force any sound out of her mouth.

The nurse spoke again, loudly, slowly, as though Nikki might be hard of hearing. "I said, about how far along do you think you are?"

"Well, I, it couldn't be . . . long, you know. I mean—" Nikki stopped, fumbling, aware that she was making no sense. She was embarrassed to feel sweat break out across her forehead. She had meant to be so nonchalant about this, so . . . adult.

"Okay. Let's try this again." The nurse sounded tired. "Do you have any idea when you got pregnant? The week, the month even?"

Nikki nodded. "May third."

May third—would she ever forget it? Would there ever again be a night when she didn't relive the whole scene before falling asleep? She could see T.J. in his tux, the restaurant crowded with balloons and flowers under the "Millbrook Junior-Senior Banquet" banner, and herself in the black dress slit to the thigh, basking in the pride of being one of the few sophomore girls invited.

Everyone migrated to the party at Lauren's house after the banquet—everyone who mattered at least—and it was there the trouble started. Nikki knew about Lauren's parties, of course. Everyone in school did. Nikki just hadn't heard about some of the finer points.

Guys Nikki had never seen before, guys who looked older than any at Millbrook High, were carrying in cases of beer, stacking them in the front hall. The tallest of them slung an arm around Lauren.

"This is one smart babe!" he announced to the others. "So how'd you get your parents out of the way, sweet thing? You must've told them some story."

He caught sight of T.J. and Nikki in the doorway and slid his arm off Lauren's shoulders, turning slowly to face them.

"Hey, what have we got here? T.J., my man, you're moving up in the world. Finally got yourself a gorgeous woman."

He looked her up and down. Nikki stiffened.

"Yes . . . yes," he said, taking inventory. "Big blue eyes, beautiful hair, great body—well, on second thought, you could take off a little there in the hips, but then I like my women soft where it matters. . . ."

"Knock it off, Jason. She's not *your woman*," T.J. said.

"Hey, these things can be arranged." He reached out and passed his hand through Nikki's shining brown hair to her shoulder, then ran it down her bare arm. "Gor-geous hair."

She jerked away from him and stepped closer to T.J.'s side.

"I said knock it off, Jason! Take your animal act somewhere else, would you?" T.J. put his arm around Nikki and pulled her close, and she leaned against the cool, smooth fabric of his tux, grateful for his presence.

It still seemed a miracle to her that T.J. even knew she was alive. Girls like Nikki—girls who actually handed in homework assignments—didn't exactly make the social scene in Millbrook, Ohio. That was especially true for the tongue-tied ones who thought too late of all the witty things they could have said, who lay in bed at night staring at the ceiling, trying to figure out what had gone wrong with another day.

Then, for no reason she could ever figure out, T.J. had turned up at her locker one afternoon. T.J., with the blond hair that made it easy to pick him out on the soccer field, as though half the girls at Millbrook High didn't already have their eyes glued on his number 10 jersey.

When he asked her to meet him after his soccer match, Nikki had been stunned at first, a little awed, but he turned out to be kind and down to earth, like a friend, really. They had been out together only three times, but she knew from the way he treated her that she could trust him. At least, that's what she had thought, until . . .

She opened her mouth a little, trying to relieve the pain of clenching her jaws together that way.

"So that means you're about eight weeks, right?"

Nikki looked at the nurse, startled, and nodded at whatever it was the woman had said. Once the scene of Lauren's party started playing in her head, she could never stop it until the end, the part she still couldn't believe.

Had it really been just the booze? Could a few drinks have changed T.J. that much?

It was later that night, when other guys from the soccer team were challenging each other to see how much beer they could down, that T.J. pulled her into the bedroom. He was breathing hard, but she knew she was safe with him. *He just wants to make out*, she had thought.

In the last two months, Nikki had replayed that thought over and over in her mind. It sounded stupid, dumber than dumb, but she never was sure what happened next. The whole scene took on an unreal quality, like the lakeshore when fog rolled in and all the landmarks disappeared.

It had started out warm and close and sweet, with some of the best kissing she had ever known. Not that she'd known that much, of course. But she had as much imagination as anyone else.

Then things started to happen, things that hurt and scared her, and she wasn't sure what to do next.

"T.J.—T.J.—" she had begun, but her words drowned against his chest. "T.J., listen—"

She felt panic building inside her, but even then she couldn't make a scene. What if she screamed at him and people ran in from the family room? What if the whole soccer team came, all those guys with their beers?

And what would T.J. think if she stopped him now? He'd never take her out again—he'd never even *look* at her again. There was no way she would risk that. *Besides, it's just one time. I'll tell him later I don't want to do this again.* The thoughts flashed through her mind in an instant, and she gave up any idea of resisting further.

T.J., who had seemed totally unaware of her for the last few minutes, finally lay still, then sat up on the side of the bed, pushing his blond hair back off his forehead. He had glanced at her once, opened his mouth to say something, then changed his mind and walked out of the room without a word.

Nikki saw him later, when she finally got herself together enough to leave the bedroom. He was back in Lauren's family room, drinking with the team as though nothing had happened. She waited the rest of the evening for T.J. to come and find her, but he never did.

Word got around sometime after midnight that T.J. was so drunk that a couple of friends were driving him home in his car.

Nobody said much to Nikki the rest of the night. She hardly knew anyone at the party anyway—that was T.J.'s crowd. Ashamed and embarrassed, she'd slipped out the back door and started walking. It was only six blocks to her house, but they were long, lonely blocks at one in the morning.

Since then, T.J. had totally ignored her, crossing the hall between classes when he saw her coming.

Suddenly, Nikki realized the nurse was still talking.

"...and of course we like to remove the POC before you're 12 weeks...so much easier on you that way...."

The voice came from far away, creeping down a long tunnel. The room started to spin. *This can't really be happening*, Nikki thought. *I'll wake up in a minute, be back in the Mazda, finishing my drive from Ohio to Gram and Grandpa Nobles'.*

"Hey, are you okay?" The nurse looked closely at Nikki. "Listen, honey, this happens to people every day. It's easy to take care of, not like when I was growing up. Terminating a pregnancy is no big deal. You just need to talk to one of our counselors. Would you like to do that?"

Nikki nodded. *Anything, just get me out of here.*

"Okay, you come on back to the waiting room with me, and I'll see if one of our gals can fit you in right now."

Nikki dutifully followed the nurse down the hall, but as soon as she was left alone in the waiting room, she bolted for the door. She knew it was childish, but she couldn't help looking back over her shoulder as she jerked the blue Mazda out of the parking lot and into traffic.

Nikki made it the rest of the way to her grandparents' house in a kind of stupor. She could guide her car smoothly enough, braking and signaling as she drove the familiar road, but all the time she was numb inside, her mind playing like a scratchy needle stuck on a record, *How could this happen to me? Nobody gets pregnant the first time. I didn't even mean for us to have sex. How could this happen to me?*

✌ *Two* ✌

IT TOOK A HALF HOUR to reach her grandparents' home from the clinic—20 minutes on the highway, then 10 more on the sandy, two-lane road that ran along the shore of Lake Michigan and into the tiny village of Rosendale. By then, Nikki could breathe evenly again, and her hands had stopped shaking. She pulled in to the driveway beside the big, blue clapboard house and gave the rearview mirror a quick glance to make sure nothing in her face would give away her secret.

At the sound of Nikki's car, her grandmother stood up from where she knelt in the flower bed beside the front porch and brushed the dirt from her shorts and sleeveless white shirt. Gram stepped over a small pile of weeds that lay limp beside her—she was death on anything that might invade her perennials—and hurried to the driveway, peeling off her garden gloves and smiling broadly. But Gallie, Gram and Grandpa's golden retriever, came bounding across the yard, stopping just short of Nikki's car. The dog planted his front paws squarely on the door of the Mazda and thrust his honey-colored head inside the open window, licking frantically at Nikki's face.

"Go on, Gallie," Nikki laughed, pushing the dog away from the window so she could open the car door.

"Nikki! Oh, honey, I'm so glad to see you! How'd it go driving up here by yourself?" Gram held her close for a moment, and Nikki smelled the fresh, sweet scent of roses mixed with the earthy smell of soil.

"Hi, Gram." Nikki kissed the soft skin of her cheek. "It was fine. Awfully hot when I left Ohio, and on the interstate, but it feels a lot cooler here."

"I don't know how people stand the heat in town. At least we get a breeze off the lake." Gram held Nikki at arm's length and surveyed her briefly. "Come on in. We'll get some iced tea, and you can tell me all about it. Just leave your things—we'll send your grandfather out for the luggage." As they walked together through the doorway to the front hall, she said, "You know, it's 3:30. We were starting to get a little concerned. When I called your mother in Ohio, she said you left at ten o'clock this morning, so we expected you nearly an hour ago."

Nikki thought fast. "I stopped in Howellsville for a while. There was a huge sidewalk sale at Leonard's, and I just couldn't resist." *And Howellsville was the safest place for a pregnancy test, since nobody knows me there*, she added to herself.

Gram laughed. "Let me go get your grandfather and tell him you're here. He's downstairs working on the dryer, but he'll be delighted at the interruption. You know how he loves fixing things." They made their way to the dining room, and Gram started for the basement stairs. "Roger!" Then she turned back to smile at her granddaughter. "I'm relieved nothing's wrong."

Nothing at all, Gram, Nikki thought. *Just this little matter of finding out I'm pregnant*. Panic washed over her again, right there in the middle of the dining room. Everything had seemed so normal while she talked with Gram. It could have been any one of the 16 summers she had spent here. But now the whole scene in the women's clinic replayed itself in her mind.

Nikki crossed to the bay window behind the table, trying to stop the thoughts that whirled inside her head. She looked out at the view she dreamed of so often during the long winter months in Ohio.

On her right, Lake Michigan, blue and shining in the hot July sun, spread as far as she could see. On her left, oak-forested dunes towered high above the house and crowded down the steep slope to a strip of white sand at the water's edge.

The gentle slap of water against the long, stone pier was the same as always—so was the fresh lake breeze, which billowed the white lace curtains at the windows and smelled faintly of fish. The tapping clips on the pier flagpole beat a steady metallic clink in the background. But in Nikki's head, the nurse's voice rang over and over, "Sure enough, honey, you're pregnant!" and in her nostrils was the antiseptic odor of the clinic.

She could hear her grandparents climbing the stairs from the basement. Nikki took three deep, slow breaths to calm herself, a trick Grandpa had taught her long ago to help her relax before stepping on stage at piano recitals.

"Nothing went wrong at all, dear," Gram was explaining as they topped the last step and came through the basement door. "She was late because she stopped at a sidewalk sale in Howellsville. Now who does that remind you of?"

"Well, mostly you, Carole," Grandpa said with a chuckle.

"You know very well I'm talking about Nikki's mother. Rachel never could drive past a sidewalk sale when she was this age."

Grandpa met Nikki in the arch of the dining room doorway and reached out to hug her close to his tall, lean frame, his plaid shirt smooth against her cheek.

"Nikki! You got here safe and sound—I was getting concerned about you driving up here alone in that car."

"Hey!" Nikki laughed. "The Mazda may not look like much, but it drives fine."

"Come on," Gram told them. "Let's take some iced tea out on the back porch where it's cool."

Walking ahead of them toward the kitchen, Gram let out a sudden shriek. "Galileo, get out of that trash! Oh, would you look at the mess all over my clean floor! You are the most irritating dog!"

When Nikki and her grandfather reached the kitchen, Gram was already on her knees, picking up chicken bones dripping with tomato sauce and muttering to herself.

"Golden retriever, my foot. You're nothing but a glorified trash hound. I have no idea why I keep you around here."

Gallie sidled up to her and draped his heavy head over her shoulder, trying to nuzzle her face while she worked.

She nudged him away. "You go on. I'm not giving in to you this time. Just go lie down in your corner."

Gallie hung his head and padded off to the rug in the corner of the kitchen.

Grandpa stood by the counter, shaking with silent laughter, and handed paper towels one after another to his wife. When at last his eyes met Nikki's, they both burst out laughing.

When the floor was finally clean again and they reached the screened-in porch off the kitchen, Nikki stretched out on the porch swing, her favorite spot since she had first been tall enough to climb into it. She lay back against the flowered cushions and set the swing into motion, pushing against the floor with one bare foot. A gentle breeze blew against her dark hair, lifting the damp strands off her forehead.

As soon as her grandparents settled themselves in the white wicker rockers facing the swing, Gallie slunk from his corner in the kitchen and lay down between them with a soft thud and a sigh. At first, Gram ignored him, but after a few minutes, she took a cracker from the plate and slipped it quietly to the dog, who wolfed it down in a single gulp.

"Well, that should show him who's boss," Grandpa said mildly, looking down into his tea.

"Oh, hush, Roger," Gram answered, embarrassed at being caught.

It was all so familiar. Any other time, Nikki would have laughed. But today, the sound of ice tinkling against the glasses brought back a thousand memories of other summer afternoons here. She swallowed hard. Her whole world was tilting crazily, turning upside down. How could everything here still be the same?

If I could just get back—somehow—to this morning. If I could start all over again, line up everything that's happened like dominoes—very, very carefully—maybe things would fall in another direction. It just wasn't real that she could be pregnant. Maybe someone mixed up the urine tests, maybe—

"Nikki! Are you all right?" Gram asked.

Nikki swung both legs to the floor and sat upright in one motion. "Sure, Gram. Why?"

"We've asked you twice about the case your father's arguing, and I don't think you heard a word."

"I'm sorry. I guess I'm more tired than I thought. I kind of drifted off for a second. Uh, Dad doesn't talk much about his cases at home. It's a murder trial, you know."

"Pretty sensational, too, from what we hear," Grandpa said. "What's really going on?"

"I don't know all the details, but I think the owner of the hardware store in Millbrook confessed to shooting his wife. Now he says he didn't do it, so Dad has to prove they got the confession improperly or something. He really wants to win this case. There's a judgeship opening up in family court, and it'll help his chances if he does."

"And your mother? How's her musical coming?"

Nikki's mother, Rachel Nobles Sheridan, taught voice classes at Millbrook Junior College and performed in local music theater during the summer.

"Fine. She did this part years ago, in college, so at least she doesn't have to learn it from scratch. They open in two weeks, so she's into a really heavy rehearsal schedule."

"Sounds like they're both pretty busy," Grandpa said quietly.

Nikki shrugged. *Like always*, she thought, but there was no need to say it. Gram and Grandpa knew what her life was like at home.

She changed the subject. "Mother told me Aunt Marta's back in the Dominican Republic for a couple weeks." Marta was younger than Nikki's mother by a decade and more of a friend than an aunt to Nikki. Her work as a musicologist involved much travel and kept her away from everyone in the family for long stretches.

"She loves it there," Gram said. "She's way up in the mountains and has to drive a couple of hours just to get to a phone."

"Isn't that kind of primitive?"

Grandpa stretched his legs out in front of him. "Well, you know Marta, always ready to try something new. Besides, she says it gives her a break from all those stuffy classrooms she teaches in the rest of the year."

"What about the Allens? Do you know when they're coming?"

"Marlene called me just this morning." Gallie got up and laid his snout tentatively on Gram's knee and looked at her with adoring eyes. Gram smiled and caressed the dog's silky ears. "She said they were all ready to leave today, but Carl had to do an emergency surgery, so they're leaving early tomorrow instead."

"I can hardly wait to see Carly and Jeff. It's what, three hours from Chicago? They'll be here by lunch, then, right?" Nikki asked.

"No," Gram said, laughing. "When Carl says they're leaving *early*, that's what he means. They'll be here by breakfast. In fact, I invited them to eat with us."

The Allens were friends who had been spending summers in the house next door at the lake for as long as Nikki could remember. Jeff Allen was a year older than Nikki, and Carly a year younger. The three of them had spent every summer together, building sand castles on the beach when they were young, then exploring the dunes and pier later on, and now, the last few years, working on perfect tans.

There were the twins, too, of course—Adam and Abby— but they were only 11 and usually under their parents' close supervision. Dr. Allen was a surgeon in a Chicago university hospital and arranged his summer schedule so he could spend July at the lake with his family. During August, he commuted, spending weekends at the lake and weekdays at his practice back in Illinois. Marlene Allen was soft-spoken, blond, with the warmest smile of anyone Nikki had ever known. Summer never officially began for Nikki until the Allens arrived.

"I'll get up early and help you make breakfast, then, Gram."

"Fine, honey, but don't feel you have to. You still look pretty tired. In fact, you seem a little thinner to me, now that I've had a good look at you. Are you losing weight?"

Nikki shrugged. "A little bit, maybe." Throwing up every morning—caused by morning sickness, she knew now—was working better than any diet she had ever tried. But it couldn't last. At some point, all the weight she'd lost, and more, would be back. She had seen women lumbering around in their last month of pregnancy, bellies and ankles huge and swollen. She shuddered. Then, suddenly, her mind began ticking off months: July, August, September. . . . The baby would be due the beginning of February. *I'll look like that—big and fat—right in the middle of my junior year.*

She stood up from the swing in such a rush that the wooden slat seat banged against the backs of her legs. "You know what I really want to do?" she asked, struggling to keep her voice calm. "Walk Gallie to the top of the dune. It's been a whole year since I saw that view. Do you mind?"

"Sure, go ahead," Grandpa said. "Gallie will love it. He didn't get his walk on the beach this morning because it was raining." He got to his feet, picked up the tea glasses and cracker plate. "I've got to get back to that dryer, anyway. There are pieces of it spread all over the basement, and your grandmother's got a load waiting in the washer."

"I won't be long," Nikki said, slamming the porch door behind her in her hurry. "Come on, Gallie, let's go." The big dog nudged the door open with his snout and cleared the four porch steps in a single exuberant leap.

Nikki had to get away, be alone, try to figure out what to do. Her throat tightened until she could hardly breathe. A baby, in February!

The whole world seemed foreign to her somehow, spinning

wildly out of control. It was as though her own body had become a stranger.

It was only 50 feet from the porch to the tree-covered dune, but the contrast never failed to amaze her. Once Nikki stepped between the trunks of the tall, stately oaks and graceful aspens, she felt the quiet of the forest take hold of her. The dune was ecologically fragile, so a boardwalk had been built over the old sand path that led to the summit. The weathered-board walkway alternated between steep ramp sections and stairs of 10 or 15 steps each. Nikki climbed as hard as she could. She forced herself to breathe slowly, steadily, trying to conquer the panic inside.

The air under the thick canopy of leaves felt cool against her skin, and green ferns, their tips curled under on themselves, crowded the forest floor. Nikki pulled herself up the final flight of stairs, ducked under the railing and crossed the sandy ground to sit beneath a massive oak tree. Here, from the crest of the dune, there was a wide view of Lake Michigan, sparkling in the sun and dotted with white sails. The leaves of the oaks that grew on the steep slope beneath her glistened in the late-afternoon sunlight, framing her view, and the mingled smell of hemlock and pungent sassafras scented the air.

Nikki sagged against the trunk of the oak and surveyed it all, trying to let the peace of the forest flow into her and calm her. This place was alive with memories. She let them crowd in—anything to hold her panicky thoughts at bay.

Over the beach, gulls wheeled and shrieked their wild, free cries. She watched them swoop to the sand, snatching up stray bits of food, and thought how she used to ride down the beach

on Grandpa's shoulders. She must have been very little, because
the ground had seemed so far away that she remembered clutching his neck in a stranglehold. He would pry her fingers loose
just long enough to get his breath but still allow her to cling till
she felt secure. Nikki always forgot her fear once he gave her
bread crusts to toss to the birds. She'd laughed at the cloud of
gulls that appeared, seemingly out of nowhere, to squawk and
scold over the chunks of bread before they even hit the ground.
When the food gave out, the gulls disappeared immediately,
leaving only the usual four or five to guard that stretch of beach.

"How do they know, Grandpa?" she would ask. "How can
they tell when to come?" He gave careful attention to her question, just as he would to the hundreds of others she'd ask during the course of each summer.

Her grandparents' love had filled up the lonely void inside
her, but for all that love, Gram and Grandpa were still . . . well,
old-fashioned. They would never understand about the party at
Lauren's house, let alone how Nikki had gotten into this mess.
If she even imagined telling them, she could picture their pride
in her draining away, their looks of hurt and disappointment.

Nikki slipped off her sandals and wiggled her feet slightly,
just enough to feel the cool, silken sand trickle down between
her toes.

Pregnant. How can I be pregnant?

*Lauren sleeps with just about every guy she dates, and nothing ever
happens to her. Besides, everybody says it's impossible to get pregnant
the first time.*

Nikki hugged her knees to her chest and leaned her forehead against them. *So how come it happened to me? How could I
be so stupid?* Tears fell to the ground between her legs, wetting
rings in the sand like tiny mud pies. It was a relief to finally be

alone and let it all out, all the fear and anger and confusion.

Gallie had been chasing chipmunks over the dunes, and now he dropped, panting, at Nikki's side. She looked up, surprised to see how low the sun hung in the sky. She unfolded her stiff legs and stood up.

She couldn't hide here forever. And somehow, while she tried to sort things out, she would have to talk and laugh and act like she always did, because her grandparents could never know. She couldn't betray her real feelings, not even for a second.

When she returned to the house, it was fragrant with the hot cinnamon smell of the peach pie Gram always made when Nikki first arrived for the summer. Eating dinner in the old dining room overlooking the beach brought back so many memories that she found herself forgetting, for whole minutes at a time, just how different things were this year.

Nikki took comfort in the sight of the heavy, cherry-red pottery plates that Gram had used for as long as she could remember, and in the quiet, measured strains of Bach that sounded from the stereo in the living room while they ate.

Grandpa broke a roll in half and spread butter evenly to the edges. "So, how's your music coming?" he asked.

"Good. Mrs. Cummings has me playing duo-piano, some stuff by Brahms, with a student from the college. We get together twice a week to practice."

"And school? Anything new there?"

Nikki helped herself to more potato salad from the heavy, cut-glass bowl. "Not much. Well, unless you count the awards assembly the last week."

"Oh, really," Grandpa said. "And did you by any chance

win one of those awards?" He waited, grinning, his fork poised in midair, and she ducked her head in embarrassment.

"Well, yeah. I got the Fine Arts Award. I played a lot in that local telethon for kids with cerebral palsy, and you know I play for choir and stuff."

"That's my girl!" he burst out.

Gram leaned over from her chair and hugged Nikki, whispering, "Good for you, honey."

"Well, we're very proud of you, I can tell you that," Grandpa said. "I just wish we could have been there. Your folks, did they . . . ?"

Nikki concentrated on her potato salad again, then shook her head quickly. "They were really busy right then. Dad's case was just starting and all. It didn't matter anyway. It was no big deal."

For a brief second, she saw Grandpa's lips close in a thin, tight line across his face, then he made a visible effort to relax. "As well as you're doing in school, I'd say you have quite a year to look forward to," he said finally.

She stared at his smiling face, and all the fear rushed back in on her. *What will the other kids say if I go back pregnant? What will T.J. say?* The thought stopped her cold. She'd never even considered T.J. finding out.

After dinner, Nikki curled up on the window seat in her room. She kicked her sandals off and hugged one of the pink-striped throw pillows close to her chest. Her back against the side wall, she looked out at the lake.

Far across the water, the sun was frozen just over the horizon, streaking the purple clouds with orange and red. She remembered sitting here as a little girl while Gram buckled her sandals on and braided her long hair into pigtails.

Now, the grown-up Nikki leaned her head against the glass and stared at the beach below. It was easy to imagine herself down there again, the waves breaking, the kids yelling, the gritty feel of the sand under her bare feet. How simple things had been back then.

All right, she told herself. *I have to figure out what to do.* Hadn't she heard it often enough from her mother? "Grow up, Nikki. Start taking control of your life." Okay, okay, so she would. She *would*.

Nikki closed her eyes to block out distractions and thought of T.J. again, how he'd walked out the bedroom door at Lauren's without a word. There was no way he would care about this baby. Their whole relationship had been just four dates. He'd never even looked her in the eye after Lauren's party.

She tried to imagine the look on his face if she told him, then realized that was absolutely out of the question. Nikki tossed the small, pink pillow at the floor, where it landed with a thud. Forget T.J.

And Carly would never understand, because she was way too smart to get herself in a mess like this. But maybe, just maybe, she could tell Jeff. Jeff, with his serious, slightly pudgy face and the glasses that always slid down the bridge of his nose. He might not be any help, but at least he'd listen.

Nikki thought back to that afternoon, to what the nurse had said. "It's easy to take care of. Of course, we like to remove the POC before you're 12 weeks ... so much easier that way." POC— products of conception—she knew that much from health class at school. Nikki shivered. She had seen the pictures of women lying with their legs spread wide apart, just a sheet over their knees. She pushed that thought away.

I hope I have enough money. She had closed out her savings account before she left home, just in case her worst fears came true.

Three hundred and sixty-seven dollars from her Saturday job at the bookstore and two years of baby-sitting lay folded carefully in the back pocket of her suitcase. Well, her worst fears *had* come true, and now she had to throw all that money right down the drain.

I wonder how much it hurts.

It doesn't matter, she told herself. *An abortion is the only way out of this. I have to do it. Right away, too, before anyone finds out, before I start gaining weight.* She had known pregnant girls at school, sure, but she also knew how the other kids talked about them. The tight panic began to rise in her throat again.

Breathe, Nikki—slow, deep breaths. O-n-e, t-w-o. She kept it up until her heart stopped pounding and she could think again.

No matter what an abortion was like, it was better than facing everyone at home, especially T.J. And her parents. Better than having everyone know how stupid she'd been. Tomorrow she would find some excuse to drive back to the clinic, and by this time tomorrow night, it would all be over.

The bedroom door creaked slightly, and Nikki opened her eyes with a start. A furry, golden snout pushed open the door.

"Gallie, come here, boy, come on," she said, patting her thigh. Gallie ambled slowly over the flowered rug and put his two front paws in Nikki's lap. Nikki wrapped her arms tightly around him and leaned her cheek against his golden head.

"You knew I needed some company, didn't you, boy?" She patted the dog and scratched his ears for a long time, watching as the sun dipped into the lake and spread its amber light across the water. The breeze was picking up now, and little pointed whitecaps peaked all over the surface of the lake. To the southwest, purple clouds massed on the horizon.

"There's a storm coming, Gallie," she said, rubbing the dog's snout gently. "Looks like a bad one."

❧ Three ❧

NIKKI SLEPT LATER than she meant to. The thunder woke her several times during the night, and each time, when she fell back asleep, it was into a deep, heavy slumber, filled with confused dreams of T.J. and urine tests and nurses who held up plastic discs with plus signs on them. And in each dream she was traveling, going to some nameless place that filled her with dread.

The clink of dishes and silverware from the kitchen window below her room finally broke through her sleep. She forced her eyes open.

I'm supposed to help make breakfast. She swung her legs over the side of the bed, grabbed a pair of denim shorts and a coral-colored T-shirt, and wriggled into them. She struggled with her long, curly hair, more unruly than usual because of the humidity, and finally tamed it into a ponytail.

And then, even running late, Nikki stole a second to lean across the window seat and look outside, because this had been her morning ritual since she was old enough to reach the window latch. She breathed in big gulps of lake air, mixed now with the aroma of coffee and sausage from the kitchen below.

The lake looks like glass, she thought, watching gulls fly low over the surface as they searched for food. Their bodies reflected in the water, as though some speeding white fish swam beneath each gliding bird.

Nikki heard the crunch of gravel as cars turned into the driveway. She listened to her grandparents call a welcome to the Allens from the kitchen doorway and turned and ran down the stairs. As she rounded the corner into the kitchen, she remembered her thought from the night before. Maybe she *could* talk to Jeff. It would help to have someone—anyone—who would listen.

"Gram, I'm sorry," Nikki began as she hurried through the door. "I overslept. What can I do to help?"

Gram dried her hands on the front of her faded, blue-flowered coverall apron and hugged her granddaughter.

"Everything's under control, sleepyhead. Your grandpa's been helping, and I think we're just about ready. He's out talking to the Allens right now. You know, on second thought, you could check and see if he remembered the orange juice. He's been turning sausages, and I'll bet he got too busy to put it on."

Nikki opened the refrigerator and took out the round-bellied glass pitcher full of juice. "You're right, Gram," she said and carried it with both hands to the table.

The Allens were walking in the door as she got back to the kitchen. Mrs. Allen came first, followed by Dr. Allen, who automatically ducked his balding head as he stepped through the doorway, then grinned at Gram and Nikki over the top of his wife's blond hair. Carl Allen never shaved on vacation. "No patients to impress at the lake," he always said, and his chin was already shaded with a day's charcoal-black growth.

"Hi, Mrs. Allen, Dr. Allen," Nikki said and hugged them both. "Carly, you got your hair cut! It looks wonderful." Carly's blond hair, always well past her shoulders, had been cut chin-length, and it framed her delicate face and sparkling brown eyes perfectly. The girls hugged, then moved aside to let in Abby and Adam. The twins jostled their way into the kitchen, deep in some private debate, as usual.

"Abby, Adam," Marlene Allen reminded them, "you're forgetting any of the few manners we've managed to drill into you."

The two stopped momentarily and looked at her, puzzled.

"Say hello," she said, clearly and distinctly.

Carl Allen rolled his eyes at Nikki's grandparents and clutched his forehead in mock despair.

As the twins said their hellos, Jeff, who had been parking the second car, ran up the steps. At least Nikki *thought* it was Jeff. She caught her breath, and her eyes opened wide.

"Jeff?" she shrieked. The whole Allen family laughed at her surprise. "You grew a foot! And your glasses—where are your glasses?"

"Contacts," Jeff answered, tapping the side of one eye and flashing his funny, crooked grin down at her. At least that hadn't changed. "And you're right, I did grow—not a foot, but five and a half inches."

Abby giggled. "Dad says he had a hormone purge."

Carl Allen choked back the laughter as long as he could, then gave in. "I said *surge*, Abby, hormone *surge*."

"Well," Adam chimed in, "whatever it was, at least now we know he's got some. Hormones, I mean."

Adam and Abby nearly doubled over laughing at the look Jeff turned on them, but they stopped abruptly when Dr. Allen's big hands settled on each of their backs and steered them toward the dining room.

"Well, you look . . . uh, you look . . . great!" Nikki stopped, confused.

Carly groaned. "Oh, come on, Nik, don't you start, too. That's all I heard this year at school." She imitated high-pitched voices: "'Oooh, Carly, when did your brother get to be so gorgeous? Can I come over and study with you sometime? Do you think Jeff will be around?' Listen, you don't know what it's like! One minute you have this brother whose major hobby is flossing, and the next thing you know, he turns into a hunk overnight. Talk about stress!" She shook her head in disgust, laughing.

Jeff covered his head with his arms, as if to fend off Carly's words. "It's a brutal world, Nik, but you know better than to listen to her. Hey, don't I even get a hello hug?"

Nikki embraced him quickly, uneasily, hardly touching him. She noted they were no longer on the same eye level. In fact, he was about the same height as T.J. now. So much for the old, comfortable Jeff. She had a sinking feeling in her stomach, watching her last chance to confide in someone evaporate into thin air.

"Well, come on in the dining room," Gram told them. "Breakfast is getting cold. Nikki, grab the muffins, please, and Carly, you take the sausages. Marlene, would you pour the coffee?"

Mrs. Allen smiled her lovely, serene smile and picked up the coffee pot.

"Carole, this is a feast, as usual. You know we love to eat with you and Roger, but I'm afraid we made a lot of work for you. You must have been up at dawn."

"This is nothing," Gram said. "I did the muffins last night and made pancake batter this morning. Rog did the rest. We're just so glad to see you and Carl." Spotting the dog out of the corner of her eye, she called out, "Gallie, don't you even think about that trash!" She picked up the wastebasket and set it on top of the counter, out of the dog's reach, and turned back to Marlene. "Your kids look wonderful. And Jeff—I can hardly believe how he's changed."

"I know. You close your eyes for just a second and they turn into adults." Marlene turned a little in the doorway. "And you, Nikki, you look just lovely. You've grown up so much since last summer."

Nikki smiled and followed the two women into the dining room where, for a few moments, everything was confusion as the men pulled up extra chairs and the women found places to set down the hot food they carried. Soon the two families settled together around the table.

"Welcome back, everyone," Grandpa said, looking around the table. "Let's give thanks before we eat." He bowed his head over his plate and thanked God for friends and family and food. Nikki didn't pay much attention to his words—she wasn't big on praying anyway—but she couldn't help feeling hopeful, hearing that calm, resonant voice. Maybe things weren't as bad as she thought. In fact, if everything went right at the clinic that afternoon, life could be back to normal in no time.

As soon as Grandpa said "Amen," the noise broke out. The sound of silverware against the red pottery plates, the conversation, and laughter filled the dining room like the breeze that gently puffed out the curtains on either side of the bay window.

"How was your year at school, Nikki?" Mrs. Allen asked, handing her the basket of blueberry muffins.

"Good. Well, good if you don't count trigonometry. I'm no better at math than I ever was."

"Me neither," Jeff groaned from across the table. "Dad made me take calculus this year, and I really blew it."

"You didn't really blow it," Dr. Allen said as he served himself pancakes from the platter Grandpa passed. "You simply disgraced the family name, that's all." He laughed and his smile took any sting from his words. He patted Jeff on the back. "Actually, it was my fault. I shouldn't have forced you into it. I just thought you might need that kind of math background for college."

"Yeah, well, thanks to that class, I may not even get into college, Dad."

"Jeff, I know you have a whole year yet to decide," Grandpa said, "but do you have any idea which college you want to go to?"

Jeff had just opened his mouth to answer when it happened.

Carly passed the plate of sausages to Nikki, and the hot, greasy smell rose in her nostrils. A wave of nausea, stronger than any she'd had yet, broke over her. She jerked her chair back, her only thought to get to the bathroom before it was too late. But in doing so, she jarred the table. The glass juice pitcher wobbled, in slow motion, then tipped on its side, sending a sweet orange flood cascading across the tablecloth.

Nikki's chair clattered backward on the polished oak floor, and for one terrible moment, she couldn't seem to untangle her legs. Then she ran for the bathroom, both hands pressed against her mouth.

She gagged and retched, her heart pounding so hard the room spun. When she was finally able to raise her head, Gram was rubbing her back gently, holding out a warm washcloth and murmuring little comforting noises. Behind her stood Dr. Allen, his brown eyes peering at her gravely.

"Here, sit on the side of the tub, honey, till you catch your breath," Gram said, stepping back to make room.

Nikki took the washcloth from her and wiped it across her flushed face as she sat down, leaning sideways against the tile wall for support.

Dr. Allen squeezed past Gram and sat down beside Nikki on the edge of the bathtub. His gentle hand felt her forehead first, then circled her wrist to time her pulse.

"What do you think's wrong, Carl?" Gram asked.

"Hard to say. Probably just some kind of a virus. It comes on suddenly like this sometimes."

Nikki grabbed at the words. "There was a lot of flu going around in Millbrook. Even my parents didn't feel good the day before I left." She listened to herself with amazement but couldn't seem to stop.

"Hmmm. Well, there you have it—unusual for this time of year, but it happens," said the doctor, still watching her carefully.

"Maybe," Gram said, "it was something I cooked last night—"

"Now don't be worrying about food poisoning. If she's been exposed to a virus, then that's the most logical explanation," he answered, his eyes on Nikki's. Suddenly, she was afraid he'd seen through her. "Can you give her a cup of tea, Carole? Weak, with a little sugar?"

"Right away." Gram left immediately, glad for some concrete way to help.

When they were alone in the bathroom, Nikki stared at the floor, afraid to meet Dr. Allen's eyes. She felt as though the word *pregnant* was stamped across her forehead. But when he spoke, his voice was quiet. "Do you think you can drink some tea, Nikki?"

She nodded, and he offered his arm for support.

In the dining room, Mrs. Allen, Carly, and Jeff were placing food back on the table, now bare of the sodden tablecloth.

Grandpa was on his knees underneath, mopping up the last of the juice that had dripped through to the floor.

Adam and Abby tried hard to keep their faces straight as Nikki sank back into her chair, but they failed. A small snorting laugh bubbled up from Adam, and to cover it he burst out, "Nik, that was really gross!" Abby joined in with giggles. Both Dr. and Mrs. Allen turned a stern gaze on the twins, and their laughter dried up immediately.

"Sorry," Adam mumbled, looking down at the table.

Nikki wished the floor would open up and swallow her whole. If she'd had any doubts about her plans for that afternoon, they were gone now. She'd leave for the Howellsville clinic as soon as she could get out of here.

Four

AFTER THE ALLENS LEFT, Gram began clearing the table. Grandpa put his arm gently around Nikki's shoulders as she stood up.

"Come on in the study with me, Nikki. You can lie on the couch and put your feet up, and I'll turn some music on. We can talk or just be quiet, whatever you want."

What she wanted was to be gone, in the Mazda, racing for Howellsville, but there was no escape. She walked with him through the living room and front hall into the book-lined study. He settled a throw pillow behind her on the satiny brown leather of the couch and went back to the living room to turn on a Mozart piano concerto. The quiet, graceful music in the background made it easier to talk.

"Which concerto is this, Grandpa? I can never remember the numbers."

"Twenty-six. The next to the last—the penultimate."

Nikki smiled to herself. Grandpa could no more resist unusual words than she could resist chocolate. He loved words almost as much as he loved his chosen subject, biology. And classical music and theology and physics. There was hardly a subject that didn't interest him. Now that he was retired, he happily passed the time between breakfast and lunch reading in all these areas.

She watched him settle into his favorite chair and pick up a book from the lamp table beside him. She realized she had never really seen him before as a separate person. He'd always just been . . . Grandpa. She knew he'd taught for years at a local college and that now his articles were in demand from journals and magazines she couldn't even understand, but she'd never really thought of him except in relationship to herself.

"How long did you teach biology at the college?" she asked.

He looked up from his book, and Nikki noticed the deep creases around his mouth. "Forty years. I started the year your mother was born. What makes you ask?"

"Just wondering. When I was little, I never really thought about what you did. You were just always here during the summers, and then when you started teaching again in the fall, I was already back in Ohio. Grandpa, remember how you used to take me for walks on the dunes? And Jeff and Carly, too? And you'd name all the trees and flowers and imitate those bird songs?" Nikki laughed suddenly. "Remember the time you found the garter snake in the backyard and let us play with it? And Mrs. Allen nearly died when she looked out the kitchen window and saw Carly holding it?"

Grandpa nodded, chuckling, and she saw where the creases in his face had come from. They were laugh lines, etched permanently around his mouth.

She thought about the year the oil spilled into the lake from a tanker. Grandpa had most of the kids in town down at the beach, cleaning gulls. He had formed them into a kind of veterinary assembly line, and he brought the birds to them for washing, birds that were muddy-black and stinking with oil, their round, flat eyes mutely imploring. With gentle fingers, he had shown the kids how to hold the birds and wipe them down with soft, detergent-soaked rags.

As she thought, the sun heated the room to a drowsy warmth. The music wove its own spell, each sparkling piano scale climbing and falling, intertwining with the orchestra, then separating to run alone again in its own direction. Nikki shut her eyes for just a second and relaxed against the soft leather. In a little while, she would make the drive into Howellsville, and this whole thing would be solved. No one would ever have to know except her—that is, unless Dr. Allen had guessed. She thought again how he had looked at her as they sat on the edge of the bathtub. Surely he couldn't tell, not just from what had happened this morning.

I hope it doesn't hurt. She pushed the sudden thought away, as she had the night before, and forced herself to concentrate on the music. *It doesn't matter anyway—at least it'll all be over.*

When she woke up a half hour later, Nikki found it easy to convince her grandparents that she needed to drive to Howellsville to shop for a bathing suit. She had a few tense moments when Gram thought she would like to go along and stop at Leonard's sidewalk sale.

"But I guess I'd better not," Gram finally decided. "I promised Arleta two cakes for her Book and Bake Sale tomorrow morning. You know that benefit sale she always has for the library? And I suppose I'd better get them done right now. Why don't you at least see if Carly can go with you?"

"She's got way too much unpacking to do, Gram," Nikki said. "You know the Allens bring half the house when they come for the summer."

"But you're sure you feel well enough to go alone?" Grandpa asked.

"I feel fine. Just a little touch of the flu, like Dr. Allen said. I was telling Gram that Mother and Dad had it, too, right before I came up here."

Just before she left, Nikki ran upstairs and felt in the back pocket of her suitcase until her fingers touched the folded wad of money. She pulled the bills out carefully, smoothed them straight, and tucked them into her purse.

That was too close for comfort, Nikki thought as she turned the Mazda off the sandy beach road and onto the highway. *That's all I would've needed—Gram coming along to a nonexistent sidewalk sale.*

She clicked on a tape, concentrating hard on the music, and tried not to think about where she was going—the sour, antiseptic smell, the jars of swabs and ointments, and the unexplained metal implements on the examining room shelves. She tried not to picture herself lying undressed on the table, her legs spread wide, tented with the ever-present white sheet.

That's enough! Stop it, now! she told herself. She reached over and twisted the volume knob so far to the right that the music crowded out everything else.

When she reached the Howellsville exit, Nikki felt relief wash over her. So it would be unpleasant. Okay. She could do it anyway. She was taking control. She'd figured out the solution to this herself, just like her parents were always telling her to. They were forever saying things like "You can't just let life happen to you, Nikki. You have to take charge, make decisions, make things work for yourself."

Well, in just a little while, she would have solved this whole problem and everything would be back to normal. Maybe, for once, her parents would have even been proud of her. But just her luck, this was one decision she could never brag about.

When she turned onto the street where the clinic was, Nikki noticed a handful of figures moving around on the sidewalk in front of the building. She looked closer. What was going on? Yesterday this place had been practically deserted.

She eased her foot off the accelerator and frowned as the car inched forward. Just as she began to nose the Mazda into the clinic driveway, her vague unease resolved into a sharp image.

Demonstrators. They were pro-life demonstrators.

That was why she had known about this clinic, Nikki realized suddenly. She used to see it on the local news three or four times each summer, in segments about abortion protests.

Nikki slid her foot across to the brake. Maybe she could wait—drive around until the demonstrators left. She checked the rearview mirror. A green pickup, riding high on oversized wheels, gunned its engine behind her, waiting impatiently to pass. Nikki swung into the clinic driveway and the truck roared by.

In the quiet that followed, the demonstrators' chant poured through her open window: "It's not a choice, it's a child! It's not a choice, it's a child!" They held large placards with words and pictures Nikki couldn't quite make out, and they marched slowly, in a ragged oval just beyond the front lawn.

Could she still get inside? What if they tried to stop her?

Take control, she thought. *I have to take control. I didn't come all this way to be scared off.*

She thought again of Dr. Allen's dark eyes watching her this morning, of Adam and Abby snickering when she threw up. She opened the car door and clutched her purse.

The demonstrators turned to watch her, and their chant seemed to grow louder. *"It's not a choice, it's a child!"*

Nikki put her head down, as though walking into a strong head wind. She fixed her eyes on the sidewalk just in front of her feet and made for the door of the clinic.

Suddenly, a heavy, gray-haired woman broke from the group and hurried to Nikki's side, walking shoulder to shoulder with her. Nikki quickened her pace, edging closer to the building side of the walkway. The woman matched her step and began to talk fast, her voice low and intent.

"Do you know what they're doing in there? They're killing babies! I know you must be in some kind of trouble or you wouldn't be here, but listen to me—this is not the solution. There's all kinds of help available to you. We have a network of homes where you can stay while you're pregnant. We have doctors who work with us, for free if you can't pay. We even have maternity clothes, if that's what you need."

Keep walking, keep walking, Nikki thought. *She can't stop you. She's not allowed to stop you.*

"Please don't let them do this to you and your child. Look, here's a picture of what the baby looks like. Take this, look at it."

Nikki hesitated. The gray-haired woman thrust brochures toward her, and Nikki automatically reached for them.

"It's not a choice, it's a child!" the chant echoed again from the group near the street. "It's not a choice, it's a child!"

Nikki stood rooted to the ground in shock. Who were these people? Why did they care what she did? She couldn't think what to say, what to do. She opened her mouth to cry "Stop it!

Leave me alone!" But her body would not obey. Suddenly, the high-pitched wail of a siren sounded behind her.

Nikki glanced back over her shoulder. Police cars were speeding up the street toward the clinic with their lights flashing. Behind them roared a white van, the letters WJRB-TV emblazoned on the side. What if they got a picture of her, standing here on the sidewalk?

"We can help," the lady beside her was saying. "We'll do anything necessary to save this child. Look, here's our number. . . ."

A cameraman climbed out of the van and slammed the door behind him. Nikki turned and ran as fast as she could back to her car.

She fell into the driver's seat, breathless. Her hands shook so violently that she fumbled her first two attempts to jam the key into the ignition. Finally, the engine turned over, and she pulled out of the parking lot as fast as she dared. *I have to get out of here before he turns that camera on.*

It was when she reached the edge of town, just as she swung the car onto the highway entrance ramp, that the nausea hit again. Nikki pulled the car onto the shoulder and bolted from her seat. She threw up over and over into the weeds alongside the road, into the gravel and broken bits of glass.

When it was over, Nikki sank back into the Mazda and leaned her head against the headrest. She couldn't drive until the shaking stopped at least a little.

After a long while, the wild hammering in her chest subsided. She clutched the steering wheel and pulled herself up straight. But when she reached down to fasten her seat belt, she was startled to see the pamphlets the demonstrator had given her lying in the passenger seat.

The brochure on top had the picture of a baby on its cover.

It wasn't like any baby she'd ever seen before, with its blue-veined eyelids closed tight, a head too big for its little body, and all of it enclosed in a transparent bubble. But it was definitely a baby.

Nikki threw her purse across the pamphlets and turned her key in the ignition.

Five

THERE WAS NOTHING LEFT to do then but go home. Nikki drove as slowly as she dared, trying to think.

This whole thing was supposed to be over by now. Instead, thanks to those stupid demonstrators, I'm no closer to solving this than I was yesterday. The weight of it dropped back across her shoulders, and for a second, she feared she would smother in the blazing July heat.

She took the exit for Rosendale, then glanced in the rearview mirror. The face she saw was white, her blue eyes dark and shadowed. If her grandparents saw her this way, there would be questions for sure.

Rosie's. She could go to Rosie's, drink a Coke, and catch her breath.

The parking lot was nearly deserted when she turned off the road in front of the faded pink sign that read "ROSIE'S GRILL—BURGERS AND MALTS."

Once the parking lot had been gravel, but years of blowing sand had buried all but a few of the stones. She climbed out of the car and squinted against the sun's glare. The sand burned the sides of her feet where it trickled into her sandals.

Beyond the small, white stucco building, Lake Michigan was wrapped in its summer-afternoon haze. Only the flimsiest breeze flipped the edges of the striped, canvas beach umbrellas that shadowed round, metal tables on the deck.

Nikki chose a table as far as she could from the two giggling little girls who were squeezing packet after packet of ketchup onto a dish of steaming French fries. She didn't recognize them, which meant they were probably vacationers, staying a week or two at Lilac Cottage, the small motel a few houses from her grandparents'.

A waitress about Nikki's age appeared eventually, her hair caught up in a ragged ponytail. "What'll you have?" the girl asked, tapping her pencil against the pale-green order pad, her eyes fixed on the beach beyond the deck railing.

"Just a Coke, please," Nikki told her.

When the drink finally came, it was served in a heavy glass mug, thick with frost on the outside. Nikki sipped the icy liquid gratefully. No one except the bored waitress and the giggling girls was around, so Nikki rested her feet on the seat of the wrought-iron chair across from her, its back edged with thin lines of rust, just like the one she was sitting in. She closed her eyes.

Now what? Howellsville has the only clinic I know of around here. So what do I do now? And how long do I have before people figure out why I'm throwing up all the time?

Until today, the nausea had been sporadic, maybe two or three times a week. But now—twice in one day—how could she hide that?

"Nikki!"

Startled, she swung her feet to the floor and swiveled around to see who was talking. Jeff Allen stood in the doorway, a tall Styrofoam cup in his hand.

"What are you doing here?" He crossed the deck to the chair beside her, bent his long frame into it, and rested one foot across his knee. "Your grandma said you were in Howellsville, shopping."

"Hi," Nikki answered, unable to think of anything else to say. She noted his easy smile and the dark hair that fell across his high forehead. She reached up and pushed her own damp, tangled hair off her face and smoothed the front of her T-shirt. Finally, she added, "I thought you were unpacking."

"Well, it doesn't take all day, right? Carly's already down at the beach." He sipped his Coke. "You feeling any better? You were kind of a mess this morning. I was surprised to hear you drove all the way into town."

"I, uh, I had to look for a bathing suit," Nikki stammered. "Besides, I'm a lot better now. Coke helps settle your stomach."

Jeff laughed. "Yeah, I know. When we were little, Dad used to give us Coke syrup if we got sick to our stomachs. I wonder if they still do that to little kids?" He paused and looked at her closely, his dark-blue eyes concerned. "You know, Nik, you're still pretty pale. Maybe you ought to stay in bed till you're over this."

Till February? Right! "I'm fine, Jeff. Don't worry about it." She reached for her Coke and knocked the condiment holder to the floor. Salt and pepper, ketchup packets, and sugar envelopes scattered across the table and around their feet.

Her clumsiness set off something inside her. She slammed her hand down on the table. "I can't believe this! Everything I do today goes wrong!"

Jeff glanced over his shoulder at the waitress and the little girls, who were all staring in their direction, and lowered his voice to a whisper.

"Nik, what's the matter? It's just some sugar and junk. Look, I'll clean it up, okay?" He picked up the condiments and stacked them in their plastic holder, glancing up at her now and then as he worked. When he finished, he slid the holder back out of the way and looked directly at her. "This is more than the flu, isn't it? I mean, you're really upset about something."

"No!" She looked away from him, her eyes tearing up. It was one of the strangest parts of this strange day, feeling edgy around Jeff, who had always been as comfortable as a pair of old shoes.

"It's just been a rotten day. I mean, I single-handedly ruined everybodys' breakfast this morning. . . ." She grabbed more out of thin air, and he kept watching her. "And I nearly had a wreck on the way home. I'm kind of shook up from that."

"What happened, Nik? You didn't get hurt, did you?"

She said the first words that formed themselves in her mouth. "Some idiot ran a red light in this big, green pickup, one of those jacked-up jobs, you know? I was just pulling out into the inter-section, and he came roaring by, honking his air horn at me like it was my fault."

I'm turning into a professional liar, she thought, but it didn't stop her from continuing.

"Lucky we had new brakes put on the Mazda before I drove up here or I never could've stopped in time. He just missed the front of my car."

"Well, no wonder you're shaky. Here—" Jeff nudged the empty metal chair back into place in front of her "—put your feet back up. Relax."

"No, it's okay. I'm fine now," she said, awkward with the concern she had earned through deceit. "I've got to get home anyway. My grandparents will wonder where I am."

They walked together to the counter to pay, then to the parking lot.

"So when do I get to see this great new bathing suit?" Jeff

asked, swinging open the car door for her.

"Bathing suit?" Nikki asked, confused.

His eyebrows arched upward. "The one you went to Howellsville to buy, remember?"

"Oh, I, uh, I couldn't find one I liked."

"Better take Carly next time. She never comes home till she finds what she's shopping for, even if it takes her all day."

"Don't I know that from experience!" Nikki added, and they laughed together. She slid into the driver's seat of her car, relieved to see that he apparently had believed her whole story.

But when she turned the key in the ignition and looked up to say good-bye, Jeff was frowning, staring in the window at the pamphlets on the front seat beside her. Following his gaze, Nikki saw what he saw—the picture of the strange little baby in the clear bubble, headlined with the words "HOW YOUR BABY GROWS." He glanced from the pamphlets to her face.

Nikki threw the car into reverse. "Jeff, I have to run. See you later, okay?" She backed out as quickly as she dared.

Later, as she turned the car onto her grandparents' street, she said out loud, "Stupid pictures!" She couldn't even throw them away at home. If anybody saw them, there would be plenty to explain. With one hand, she picked up the brochures and jammed them into her purse.

What right did those people have to interfere in her life anyway? Because of them, she was right back where she'd started.

The house seemed to drowse in the midafternoon heat, its windows curtained and shaded against the intense sun. Nikki stepped inside quietly, thankful for the cool air and the silence. The sweet smell of Gram's baking filled the front hall.

From behind the closed study door came the muted clicking of the computer keyboard. Grandpa must be working on another article. She tapped on the door with one fingernail, opened it a crack, and looked around the edge.

"Hi. I'm back."

Grandpa glanced up from the open books and notebooks that covered the desktop and smiled at her.

"Good," he said. "Did you get what you need?"

"Well, not exactly, but I can go back another time."

"And your stomach? How's it feel?"

"So-so," she said. "I think I'll go lie down for a while."

"Your grandmother's taking a nap. She said she had a headache."

"I'll be quiet."

Nikki stopped in the kitchen first, lured by the warm vanilla scent. Four single cake layers cooled on the counter. She lifted the waxed paper that lay on top of one and inhaled deeply. Her stomach growled, and for the first time that day, food sounded like a good idea.

She pulled open the refrigerator door and looked inside. There was leftover tuna salad and a plastic milk container. She ate cautiously, afraid she might trigger another episode of nausea, then made her way quietly up the stairs.

From the top step, she could see through the partly open door into her grandparents' bedroom. The window shades were pulled almost to the sills, shutting out most of the sunlight but open enough to catch any breeze that wandered in off the lake.

Gram lay curled on her side of the big bed, a book open beside her on the white chenille bedspread. Her hand, relaxed in sleep, spread over the pages, and her silver-framed reading glasses lay fallen on the flowered carpet beside the bed. Nikki tiptoed in, retrieved the glasses, and laid them on the bedside table. Standing so close, she could see Gram's cheeks were flushed and rosy from the heat and could hear her even breathing.

Nikki felt a sudden sharp pang. She could curl up right now in the great walnut rocker beside the bed and spill the whole story. Gram would open her eyes slowly at first, but once she was awake, she'd listen intently, hearing even the words Nikki couldn't bring herself to say. And then the soft creases around her mouth would tighten and, even though she smiled, there would be hurt and disappointment in her brown eyes.

Nikki turned and tiptoed down the hall to her own room, careful to avoid the boards that creaked.

Her bedroom door shut with a soft click. What now? Nikki caught sight of herself in the old dresser mirror. She turned in profile, pulling her T-shirt taut against her abdomen, and stopped short. There was a slight bulge.

Am I starting to show already? She whirled around in a panic and checked again from the other side. This time her stomach was flat. It had only been the wavy glass, distorting her image like a fun-house mirror.

She sprawled across the bed, weak with relief, and lay staring at the ceiling. She could hear her mother saying, "Quit see-sawing, Nicole. The women who get somewhere in life are the ones who take charge, make decisions for themselves." Well, she'd tried, hadn't she? As usual, it hadn't worked.

Her parents didn't have a clue that most of her indecisiveness came from fear of their disdain. Even when she did her best, her decisions were usually "immature" or "hasty" or, their favorite, "not well thought through." There was a whole list of words they trotted out on a minute's notice.

Well, they aren't around now to sit in judgment. They never even have to know. This is my decision and mine alone. And I will figure it out.

Tomorrow, she would go back to the clinic. Those demonstrators couldn't be there every day. They had to have jobs and other things to do. She didn't know what excuse she'd give her grandparents for driving back to Howellsville again, but she would think of something. She'd use some ingenuity for a change. And she'd get this taken care of once and for all. Then, surprising herself, Nikki started to cry.

She rolled over on her stomach, arms clutched around the pillow, where she buried her head to hide the sound, and cried until she felt hollow and empty.

It was the flapping window shade that woke her. The breeze off the lake had risen and cooled the room slightly, but the vinyl shade snapped sharply against the window frame with each small gust of air.

Nikki sat upright on the rumpled bed and rubbed her eyes, then grimaced at the sight of mascara on her fingers. Now she would have to redo her whole face.

Her purse lay on the bedspread where she'd tossed it, the pro-life pamphlets spilling out of it. Nikki swore softly under her breath. *I've got to get rid of these things.* But she couldn't resist picking one up.

She studied the cover picture. *So that's what it looks like,* she thought. Inside the brochure was another picture, a close-up this time. The baby's thin, delicate arms stretched out in front as though it were reaching—for what? She studied the tiny hands, the minute fingers and thumbs, the translucent ivory skin.

The headings said, "5 to 9 DAYS," then "14 DAYS, 30 DAYS, 45 DAYS." She knew she should close the brochure, throw it away, but she was looking for one heading in particular.

"EIGHT WEEKS: Child now well-proportioned, about one and an eighth inches. All organs present; heart beats steadily. Taste buds forming." Nikki bit hard at her lower lip. "NINE WEEKS: Five major subdivisions of the brain have now formed. Baby bends fingers around object placed in palm; sucks his thumb. Fingernails are forming."

The pamphlets slid to the floor as Nikki stretched her hands out in front of her, flexing her own slender fingers, her polished nails glistening. She was so proud of those nails. "Quit peeling your fingernails, Nicole." That was the eleventh commandment in her house. "Your hands look like a war zone," her mother was always complaining. Well, not anymore. Her nails had somehow survived even yesterday's news at the clinic.

She frowned and folded her fingers in a tight fist against her palms so she wouldn't be tempted now. *It's true*, she thought, *what Dad says when he sees news coverage of abortion protests*. She hated it that he was right, but he was. "Cheap propaganda," he always sneered, "designed to scare women with a lot of gruesome pictures that appeal to their emotions, not their minds. It ought to be against the law."

Relief flowed through her. *Propaganda. This stuff probably isn't even true. Who knows where they got these pictures? Probably made them up somehow. They're just trying to scare people.*

She bent over and picked up the pamphlets. Quickly, methodically, she ripped them into tiny, unreadable rectangles.

Outside her door, the phone on the hall table rang. She ran to answer it, stuffing the bits of paper into the pocket of her shorts.

⤳

That evening, after dinner, Nikki walked with Jeff and Carly down the beach to the pier. Carly was already sporting a sunburn from her afternoon on the sand. She rubbed gingerly at the nape of her neck, where the Chicago Cubs T-shirt, one of her large collection of shirts depicting her favorite team, chafed her red skin.

"Dad's having a fit," Carly complained, picking up shells and tossing them into the quiet waves that lapped the shore. "I didn't use sunscreen, and I got the whole skin-cancer lecture at dinner. The unabridged version. You should have a doctor for a father, Nik. It's a real picnic."

"So why didn't you use sunscreen?" Nikki asked. "You're so fair—you know you always fry in the sun."

"Because you have to have brains to think of that," Jeff put in. He ducked the shell Carly tossed at him.

"Because," she said, "a burn's better than nothing. At least I won't be white as a ghost for the next day or two. You're lucky, Nik, you always look tanned with that olive skin of yours."

It's nice to have one good point, anyway, Nikki thought, watching Carly's picture-perfect figure ahead of her on the beach.

They climbed the tumbled gray boulders that were piled in the channel as a base for the pier. Beneath the high-tide line, the huge stones were smooth, algae-covered, and slick. Nikki's sandal slid on a patch of the algae, and Jeff reached out quickly to steady her.

"Oh, sure, catch Nikki and just let me fall in the water," said Carly, fighting to keep her balance on the slippery rocks. "Who needs sisters, right?" When she reached the walkway, she turned and grinned at Nikki. "It's the story of my life. I just hope there're some guys around here this summer, so I can get some attention, too."

"There you go. Your prayers have been answered." Jeff nudged his sister with an elbow and nodded at a group of gangly boys who couldn't have been more than 10 years old coming toward them on the pier. The kids wore wildly patterned shorts and flopping, untied basketball shoes. And they were alternately pretending to push each other into the water and catcalling the boats that passed up and down the channel. "Some real men for you, Carly."

Carly snorted. "Two billion guys in the world, and I get you for a brother. Now there's a deal!"

When they reached the far end of the pier, they sat for a long time beneath the pulsing flash of the lighthouse, dangling their bare legs in the spray of the waves. Most of the walkers had already gone back to the beach, leaving the pier deserted except for fishermen. The sun, which had been inching toward the horizon, suddenly gathered speed and slipped behind the water. In that instant, the lake and clouds turned the same shade of slate gray.

All across the water, twinkling lights began to bob, marking boats on their way back into the channel. One by one, the boats cut back their raucous motors as they approached the channel entrance, then glided slowly past the pier, with only a muffled low throb, more felt than heard.

With strong, straight fingers, Jeff pried loose the little pebbles embedded in the crumbling concrete of the pier and dropped them into the water beneath their feet. Now that the sun had set, the breeze dwindled to nothing. The waves made only the faintest slapping sound against the pier, and Jeff's small missiles fell with a hollow *plunk* through the clear surface of the water to the dark depths below.

"Dad's going down to Saugatuck tomorrow to get the boat out of storage," he said. "He's planning to take us all out to watch the fireworks from the water again."

"That's right—tomorrow's the Fourth," Nikki said. *That means the clinic in Howellsville will be closed. Now what am I supposed to do?*

"Remember last year, Nikki?" Carly brushed a moth off her leg. "I loved that—the lights reflecting on the water and all."

But Nikki hardly heard her. Fourth of July had always been one of the highlights of summer vacation, but this year, it meant she'd have to wait even longer to get back to the clinic. Nikki felt as though she carried a weight inside her, a weight as heavy as the huge boulders supporting the pier.

"Look," Carly said, pointing upward. "The first star. Remember when we were really little? And we used to wish on it?"

Nikki looked up at the star, and something twisted inside her. She would give anything, anything at all, to get back to the time Carly spoke of, when the wishes and the problems had been equally simple. But no amount of wishing would bring her a miracle this time.

Six

WHEN NIKKI LET HERSELF IN the kitchen door, the house felt quiet and empty without Gallie pressing against her legs, wagging his feathery tail and waiting with lowered head for his ears to be scratched. It meant Gram and Grandpa were already in bed, the dog asleep in his basket in their room.

Nikki took a glass of orange juice and a bagel to the screened porch and curled up on the cushions of the porch swing, staring out at the night. She pushed her toe against the floor and started the swing swaying, creaking, through the thick, sweet honeysuckle air.

Slowly, hesitantly, the blackness resolved itself into parts—dark sky above, lighter lake beneath, the horizon marked by the pinpoint lights of barges crawling through the darkness. Far away, the low, mournful throb of the foghorn sounded.

Nikki shivered at the loneliness of the sound. She rubbed the goosebumps that broke out on her bare legs in the cool night air, and when she did, her hand brushed the bulge of the torn brochures in her pocket. It was hard to push away the thought of what she had seen there.

Thousands of people have abortions every year, she thought, gliding back and forth through the smooth darkness. *They can't be killing babies that look like the ones in the brochures. People wouldn't do that. They couldn't.*

Her father had to be right—the pro-life people were using scare tactics, pictures that were misleading somehow. She thought of the day, years ago, when Grandpa had taken her and Jeff and Carly to the Grand Rapids museum. There had been a whole display there about how babies grow. She knew that much, but she couldn't remember any details, no matter how hard she tried. She, Jeff, and Carly had been far more interested in the Indian tepee in the next room than in pictures of babies.

Nikki closed her eyes. She tried to imagine what was inside her looking like the picture in the brochure. Would it feel pain when she had the abortion?

It doesn't change anything. It can't. There's no way I'm having this baby. She stopped the swing in mid-arc and made her way up the stairs to her room. When she crawled into bed, the sheets felt cool and smooth against her bare legs. But as soon as she closed her eyes, the pictures from the brochure danced through the darkness, stark white against the black of her eyelids.

"You have to start making your own choices, Nicole, taking charge of your life," her mother's voice echoed in her mind. "You have to grow up sometime." She flipped onto her stomach and pulled the pillow over her head to shut out the words.

Much later, Nikki found herself struggling to surface from a deep sleep. She propped herself up on one elbow, listening, trying to identify what it was that had wakened her.

She heard floorboards creak, then a muffled thump, as though something heavy had fallen somewhere in the house, then a strange, strangled-sounding cry: "Nikki. *Nikki! Come here! Nikki, hurry!*"

Nikki threw back the covers and ran down the hall toward her grandparents' room. She stopped in the doorway, frozen.

At the foot of the bed, outside the dim pool of light cast by the bedside lamp, Grandpa knelt on the floor, cradling Gram's head in his lap.

One of her legs bent sideways at an impossible angle. One arm dangled limply over Grandpa's knee. Gram's yellow-print nightgown spread around her like a poppy on the rose-colored carpet, the white skin of her legs marked with blue-purple veins.

"Nikki, call 911!" Grandpa ordered, his voice tight. "Get an ambulance."

She stood staring, rooted to the ground, unable to move.

"Nikki, now! *Call now!*"

His words snapped the spell that held her. She turned and grabbed the phone from the small mahogany table in the hall.

"And as soon as you're done, call Carl Allen," Grandpa ordered. "Tell him to come right away!"

Her shaking fingers hit 912. She disconnected, tried again, and this time got it right. Within seconds, she had given the dispatcher directions.

When she dialed the Allens, the phone rang three times, then four.

She looked over her shoulder at the nightmare tableau behind her. Grandpa's head bent close to Gram's white face. His wrinkled hands stroked her hair, and his lips moved with words Nikki couldn't hear.

Five rings. Six.

Where are they? Why don't they answer?

Gram's eyes, wide and startled-looking, locked on Grandpa's face, as though onto a lifeline.

"Hello?"

"Dr. Allen! Dr. Allen, this is Nikki. Next door. Gram's hurt— I mean, she's sick. She's on the floor and—just—can you come right away? We need you."

"Be right there," he answered, and Nikki ran downstairs to unlock the kitchen door.

He was already sprinting across the gravel drive between the houses, his bag in hand. The dark, curly hair on his chest showed through the unbuttoned shirt he'd thrown on over a pair of gray jersey shorts. His feet looked strangely naked, thrust into dress shoes with no socks.

"Upstairs . . . they're . . ."

He nodded, brushing past her with only a brief pat to her shoulder. Nikki heard the soft, hollow thud of his footsteps on the stairs. She turned to follow him, then remembered the ambulance was coming. She ran to switch on the porch light and unlock the front door, then dashed back up the stairs.

Dr. Allen was kneeling on the floor beside Gram, his back to the hall, his stethoscope moving painstakingly across her chest. Nikki stood just behind him, watching every move.

When at last he'd heard enough, the doctor coiled the stethoscope's black tubes over the metal bell, stuck it back in his bag, and bent closer over Gram.

"Carole, I just need to see here for a minute. . . ." He spoke softly, keeping up a reassuring undercurrent of words, as he gently pulled down her lower lids and peered into her frightened eyes. "Good, good, okay, that's good. Now, Carole, can you say anything for me? Anything at all? Any sound?"

Gram stared at him.

Nikki felt terror well up in her chest. *Answer him. Answer him!*
She stepped closer and saw that one side of Gram's mouth
was moving slightly, wobbling without direction. The other side
hung down, lips limp and slack in her white face. At last, she
closed her eyes, weak from effort.

The high, thin wail of a siren wound through the open window, growing sharper as it neared the house. Nikki turned
toward the sound and was startled to see Mrs. Allen standing
quietly in the bedroom doorway, a long, green robe wrapped
around her, her blond hair pushed back with a headband. She
held out her arms, and Nikki went to her.

"What's going on? Why can't she talk?" Nikki whispered.

Marlene Allen hugged her close and whispered against her
hair. "It looks like she might have had a stroke."

"You mean she'll never be able to talk again?" Tears started
down Nikki's cheeks as she stared at her.

"Oh, no, Nikki. Most stroke patients recover their ability to
speak, at least partially. But it's too early to tell. We have to wait
and see."

"Well, just tell me this. Do you think she's going to die?"

Mrs. Allen squeezed her shoulders gently and hesitated for
a second. "Nikki, listen. Lots of people live through strokes and
recover very well."

The doorbell rang. Mrs. Allen turned and called, "Up here!
Come right up the stairs."

The scene blurred in front of Nikki. Dr. Allen gave orders,
directing the ambulance attendants. Everyone seemed to know
exactly what to do, flowing quickly, efficiently around the island
where Gram lay—everyone but Gram, who didn't move at all.

Finally, the attendants lifted her gently onto the stretcher, fastened the safety straps, and started for the stairs. Nikki broke from Mrs. Allen's hug as they passed by, and she bent over her grandmother.

"Gram ... Gram, I love you!"

There was no response.

Grandpa followed immediately behind the stretcher. He stopped to hug Nikki briefly, then turned to Mrs. Allen.

"Marlene, would you ... ?"

She held up one hand. "Roger, you don't even need to ask. We'll take care of everything here."

"But I'm going with you," Nikki cried.

"Honey, listen." Grandpa laid a hand on her shoulder. "It's better if you stay here, get some sleep. It's going to be a long night. They think she's had a stroke, but there will be lots of tests. I'll call as soon as we know anything for sure." He kissed her forehead quickly, then hurried down the stairs.

"He's right, Nikki," Dr. Allen said. "There's no point in your coming and just sitting there all night. We'll call the minute we know ..." He leaned across her and hugged his wife.

"See you, hon."

And then they were gone.

Nikki leaned against the frame of the hall window and watched the attendants maneuver the narrow, white stretcher into the yawning back of the ambulance. The brightly lit interior, crowded with shiny, silver dials and knobs, looked like a small surrealistic spaceship in the soft summer night. Crickets chirped on, uninterrupted, but as Nikki watched Grandpa hoist himself into the ambulance beside Gram and Dr. Allen, and saw the double doors close and heard the siren begin its wail again, she felt a strange darkness close around her.

❧ *Seven* ❧

AFTER THE AMBULANCE LEFT, Mrs. Allen and Nikki straightened the bedroom together. As they made the bed and folded the afghan, Mrs. Allen answered as many of Nikki's questions about strokes as she could, then she urged her to spend the rest of the night at the Allens'.

"Why don't you just grab your pillow and robe?" Mrs. Allen said. "You know we have plenty of room."

Nikki started to agree, then hesitated. What if she got sick first thing in the morning at their house? She felt the shock of being pregnant all over again. For the last hour, she had been so wrapped up in Gram's problems that she'd completely forgotten her own.

"Thanks . . . but I think I better stay here." Throwing up two mornings in a row in front of the Allens would surely give her away.

"I could make you some tea, and we could talk some more," Mrs. Allen offered. "I hate to leave you here alone."

"I'm not really alone. Gallie's here, and I feel safe with him around. I just think I'd rather sleep in my own bed."

Mrs. Allen looked doubtful.

"I'll be fine, really," Nikki insisted. "I'll call you if I need anything."

Mrs. Allen hugged her. "You come over first thing for breakfast then, all right?"

Nikki nodded.

"I'll lock the door downstairs on my way out. And Nikki, try not to worry too much. Things have a way of working out."

When she was gone, Nikki felt an uneasy silence descend on the house. She looked around her grandparents' room and tried to envision how Gram had looked, napping on the bed that afternoon, but all she could see was the white-faced stranger on the stretcher.

How fast things changed.

Gallie lay on the carpet at Gram's side of the bed.

"Come on, boy," Nikki said. "Come on down to my room."

But the dog refused to budge, no matter how Nikki coaxed and patted him. Finally, she gave up and walked down the hall alone.

She crawled into bed and turned off the bedside lamp. Then she switched it back on, got up, and pushed in the lock on the bedroom door.

Back in bed, she lay staring into the darkness. She thought of Gram in the kitchen after dinner, frosting the double-layer cakes, laughing as she handed chocolate-covered beaters to both Nikki and Grandpa to lick.

"You two may get the beaters," she had said, "but the cook gets the scraper, and that's the real gold mine!"

Nikki looked at the ceiling, remembering how Gram had scraped the last of the frosting from the bowl and ate it with obvious delight. In fact, she did everything—baking, working in the garden, puttering around the house—with delight.

Oh, Gram, what are you thinking? Does it hurt? What's it like, not being able to talk? In every memory of her that Nikki could bring back, Gram was talking or singing, never silent. How could she live without being able to talk?

If she lived.

God, please, please help her to live! Nikki stopped, searching her mind for the prayers she used to say at bedtime. It had been years since she decided that praying was fine for people like Gram and Grandpa, or Carl and Marlene Allen, but not for her. Not after all the times she had pleaded with God to make things better between her parents and nothing had happened. And now, all these years later, "Now I lay me down to sleep" was the only prayer she could recall. She tried again to make up her own.

God, please help Gram. I'll do whatever You want. What *did* He want from people anyway? She promised the only thing she could think of. *I'll go to church every Sunday—just let her get better.*

Nikki cried for a long time then, alone in the dark, thinking of Gram lying so still, wide-eyed and frightened, on the bedroom floor—Gram, always so independent and resourceful, bundled into the ambulance like a sack of potatoes.

When her tears finally dried and Nikki hovered at the point of drifting off to sleep, another thought came suddenly. With both Gram and Grandpa at the hospital, it would be easy to get away to the Howellsville clinic as soon as it reopened. There would be no need to lie or make excuses this time, since nobody would be around.

Shame overwhelmed her. *Pure sleaze, Nikki, that's what you are. Gram's probably dying, and all you can think about is how this makes things work out better for you.* Disgusted, she punched her pillow into shape, rolled over, and shut her eyes.

The phone rang, jarring Nikki, but she fell back asleep almost immediately. It rang again, and this time the sound wove itself into her dream. Everyone was running to answer it: Gram in her yellow-print nightgown, her mouth moving soundlessly; Jeff, the new Jeff, with contacts and a slender, six-foot body, who suddenly turned back into the old Jeff, pudgy, glasses slipping down his nose as he ran; and a nurse, waving a huge, round, white sign in Nikki's face as she galloped by, shouting "Pregnant! Pregnant! Pregnant!"

As the phone continued to ring, Nikki broke out of the nightmare with an effort and lurched into the hall, still unsteady from sleep. She picked up the receiver.

"Grandpa? How's Gram?" she managed, her tongue moving sluggishly, refusing to wake up. Across the hall, Gallie lay in the doorway of her grandparents' room, staring down the stairs.

"This is your mother, Nicole, not your grandfather. Good morning." The voice was like silk from years of vocal training, slippery smooth. "Nicole, are you there?"

"Yeah. Yes, I'm here, Mother. Did Grandpa call you? Do you know what—?"

"We just got off the phone with him, and we'll be leaving as soon as we can pack."

"Leaving? What . . . where?" Nikki propped the phone between her ear and shoulder so that her hands were free to rub both eyes.

"Nicole, are you awake?"

"Uh, not exactly. What time is it?"

"Seven o'clock."

"Oh. So where . . . you mean you're coming up here?" Nikki felt the nausea start, along with a headache. She leaned back against the wall and sank down slowly until her bottom reached the floor.

"We're leaving as soon as we can, probably in an hour or so. Your father has to have Judge Connors grant a continuance so he can stay there through next week, if necessary. And I have to make arrangements at the theater. This is our last week of rehearsal. Fortunately, I know the part inside out, but the others in the cast . . . "

"That's too bad," Nikki answered perfunctorily. "Listen, what did Grandpa say about Gram when he called? How is she? Was it a stroke?"

"One question at a time, Nicole. Your grandmother has had a serious stroke. They're trying to dissolve the blood clot with medication, and they're not sure how much damage there has already been to the brain, but they know it's quite a bit." Her words were clipped and curiously detached.

How strange, Nikki thought. *This is her own mother she's talking about, but it sounds like something she read in the paper.*

"So," her mother continued, "we'll be there by noon, most likely. We'll come by the house and pick you up and go in to the hospital together, so make sure you're ready on time. We won't want to wait."

The phone rang again as soon as she rested it in its cradle. This time it was Grandpa.

"Nikki? Good morning, honey. I thought you'd be at the Allens, so I called there first. Are you all right?"

"I'm fine, Grandpa. How's Gram?"

"Well, they know now that it was definitely a stroke."

"Yeah, Mother told me."

"Oh, you've already talked to her. Then you know the details, right? At this point, we're praying her brain doesn't start to swell. Carl says that happens sometimes after a stroke, and it could cause more damage. But all we can do is wait and see." His voice was husky with exhaustion.

"Grandpa, can she . . . can she say anything yet?"

The line went silent for a moment. "Nikki, didn't your mother tell you? Honey, your grandmother's not conscious. She's . . . she's slipped into a coma." His voice wavered on the last word.

"A coma? Oh, Grandpa!"

"Now listen, honey. Carl tells me it's fairly common for this to happen. Hopefully, it won't last long. This is a time for faith, Nikki. Don't give up now."

"Oh, Grandpa, I can't believe this is happening." She pulled a crumpled tissue from her pocket and blew her nose.

"Nikki? Are you still there?"

"Yeah. Listen, Grandpa. My parents want me to wait till they get here at noon, then come in to the hospital with them, but I want to drive in now so I can be with you and Gram."

"Actually, it's probably better to do what your parents asked. Your grandma's scheduled for tests all morning, so she won't even be here in the room. While they do the tests, Carl and I are both going to try to catch a little sleep on the waiting room couches."

Nikki agreed to wait for her parents, then said good-bye. She replaced the receiver and wiped her eyes with the back of her hand. "A time for faith," he had said, but faith in what? In who? *It's simple for you, Grandpa. You grew up in such a different world, one where God was a sure thing. But sometimes I'm not even sure there is a God.*

She got up off the floor and went to Gallie's side. "Come on, Gallie." She scratched the dog's soft, golden ears. "It's time to go out."

The big dog raised his head for more petting, looking at Nikki with sad brown eyes, but as soon as the petting stopped, he heaved a great sigh and dropped his head back down onto his front legs. His graceful feathered tail thumped twice, then lay still. Nikki had the distinct impression she had been dismissed.

Nikki had just stepped out of the shower when she heard a knock at the kitchen door. She wrapped a towel around herself and trailed wet footprints down the hall to the side window of her bedroom.

Jeff Allen slouched on the kitchen doorstep below, his gray fishing hat pulled down over his forehead and his shoulders hunched forward against the fine drizzle falling from the overcast sky.

"I'm up here, Jeff," she called. "What do you need?"

He looked up, shielding his eyes with one hand. Even in that crazy hat, with the drizzle running down his face, it was impossible to miss the high cheekbones and cleft chin, the thick dark lashes that framed his eyes. Nikki pulled the towel tighter around her and inched back a little from the window so he could see only her face.

"Mom wants to know if you're ready for breakfast. She's been trying to call you for quite a while, and the muffins are getting cold."

"Sorry, I was in the shower and didn't hear the phone."

"So—" he spread his hands wide, palms up "—what should I tell the chef?"

"I need about 15 minutes. Is that okay? Tell her I'm sorry about the muffins."

"Hey, it's not the end of the world." He smiled and turned to go, then looked back up at the window. "Nik?"

"Yeah?"

"I'm really sorry about your grandma. I've been trying to think of something I could say that would help, but I'm not too bright that way. And Nik?" He wiped the rain out of his eyes. "I would've been here if I'd known—I slept through the whole thing."

Nikki blinked hard and smiled down at him. "Thanks, Jeff. It's all right. Listen, I'll see you in a few minutes, okay?"

Breakfast at the Allens almost made Nikki feel things were back to normal. Only Adam spoiled the illusion.

"Man, I wish I'd seen that ambulance with the lights and siren and everything," he said through a mouthful of muffin. "That must've been really cool."

Marlene Allen turned one of her famous looks on him, the ones Jeff always said could "stop Genghis Khan in his tracks," but it was Abby who summed things up before anyone else could speak.

"You always say the dumbest things, Adam." She turned back to the rest of the family with her hands planted firmly on her hips. "I guess it's just one of his idiot syncrasies."

Everyone except the twins broke up laughing, and Jeff shook his head. "The wonder child strikes again," he murmured.

"Are you by any chance trying to say *idiosyncrasies*, Abby?" Mrs. Allen asked, managing to sound kind even through her correction.

"Well," Carly put in, "you have to admit, her version fits Adam better than yours, Mom."

This is what a family should be like, Nikki thought as she picked at her blueberry muffin and pushed the scrambled eggs back and forth across her plate. *Having fun, laughing together—the way I always wished our family would be.* Then her thoughts switched back to the now-familiar rolling in her stomach.

I absolutely will not throw up here. If I do, I might as well wear a sandwich board saying I'm pregnant. She watched carefully for a time when she could leave without being rude and managed to make it home just in time to be sick again in the downstairs bathroom.

⤥

"**C**'mon, Gallie."

The dog, still stretched across the doorway of Gram's room, watched Nikki's movements through impassive eyes. When Nikki placed a bowl of water in front of him, he nosed it politely but refused to drink. When she offered dog biscuits, he turned his head to the side and stared at the bedroom wall.

"Gallie, listen. Gram will come back. She'll be well in no time."

I hope.

"You've got to eat and drink something." Nikki pushed the water bowl aside and lowered herself, cross-legged, to the floor in front of the dog, stroking his thick, reddish-gold fur. He licked her hand halfheartedly, but it was clear he did it only out of duty.

"Gallie, come on!" She tried to speak sharply, with authority, but when the dog lifted his eyes, Nikki saw in the soft brown depths a grief that, on some other level, matched her own.

"Well, I've got to get you outside, no matter how upset you are." She got to her feet and snapped the thin leather leash onto his collar. She had expected him to balk, but he followed her downstairs quietly. *I'd rather go than argue about it*, his lowered head seemed to say.

Outside, the drizzle had stopped, but the sky remained the flat gray color of gravel. The rain-drenched honeysuckle along the side of the house permeated the air with its heavy sweetness. When Nikki unsnapped Gallie's leash at the edge of the dune, the dog plodded quietly by her side, showing no interest in the squirrel trails that usually tantalized him.

The forest was silent, the wood of the boardwalk colored a dark, wet charcoal. There was only the faint sound of the waves breaking on the shore far below and the occasional *drip, drip, drip* of rain off the wet leaves.

Nikki climbed slowly to the summit of the dune and sat down on the lightest-colored step she could find, one partially shielded by the leaves of the great oak overhead. Hemlocks grew here and there throughout the forest, dark-green dripping spears of color against the spreading canopy of red oak and beech. Gallie edged closer to Nikki, trying to sit on the step beside her. Nikki inched over, making room, and the two of them sat side by side in silence.

The chill gray of the sky seemed to press down on her. For a time last night, in the tenseness of Gram's stroke, the worry about being pregnant had been crowded out of her mind. But now it seemed as though the burden had doubled. Even the ferns—the great cinnamon ferns, their fuzzy cinnamon-stick spikes thrust up from their centers, and the delicate, lacy fronds of the lady ferns—seemed to sag with dampness. Every plant dripped and hung low to the forest floor.

"Not even a squirrel to chase this morning, huh, boy?" Nikki rubbed her chin over Gallie's furry head. "Well, just wait. There'll be plenty of excitement when Mother and Dad get here. First, we'll hear how postponing Dad's trial will really screw things up for him. Then we'll hear how Mother is missing her last, *and most important*, week of rehearsal. And chances are they'll manage to get in at least one major fight while they're here. And Grandpa will have to put up with it all while he's worried sick about Gram."

Gallie moved his head impatiently beneath Nikki's chin, seeking more attention, and Nikki caressed his long, silky ears.

At last, she stood to her feet. "They'll be here soon, Gallie. We'd better get going."

Nikki jogged home with Gallie loping easily by her side. She thought she had left enough time to get back before noon, but there in the driveway sat her father's Chrysler, its sleek, sage-green shine unmarred by any dust from the four-hour trip.

Abby and Adam were eyeing the car from the steps of their front porch, where they sat licking Popsicles.

"Hey, Nik, cool car," Adam called as she sprinted up the walk. "When'd you get it?"

Nikki let his question hang. "Do you know what time it is?" she called back.

Abby squinted at her watch. "It's 12:14 and 30 seconds," she answered, her open mouth glinting with braces.

Oh, great. Now they can say it for the millionth time: Nikki, you're always late! She slammed the front door behind her and bent to unsnap Gallie's leash.

"Mother? Dad?" She heard voices coming from the kitchen

and walked toward them. Rachel Sheridan stood with her back to the doorway, talking on the phone, one slender hand threading its way through her curly, wheat-colored hair again and again. Even from behind, her figure, encased in tan stretch pants and a matching silk tunic, was flawless.

David Sheridan lounged against the kitchen counter, cutting his nails with the engraved clippers on his key ring. He glanced up when Nikki entered the room and acknowledged her presence with a slight lift of his eyebrows. Nikki went to his side, and he slipped the key ring back into the pocket of his chino pants, smoothing the V-neck cotton sweater down over them and folding his arms in front of him.

He nodded toward his wife. "She's talking to your grandfather. He called just before you walked in. Sounds like another emergency."

"Oh, no! Dad, Gram didn't . . . die, did she?" Nikki felt as though the breath was being squeezed out of her.

"Calm down, Nikki. If she died, it would hardly be an emergency, would it? I mean, the whole situation would be resolved then."

The teakettle jiggled and hissed, then slid into a shrill whistle. Mr. Sheridan turned to lift it from the stove.

"Want some tea?" he asked.

"No. I want to know what's going on with Gram!"

At the other end of the counter, Nikki's mother turned and frowned them into silence.

"Mmm-hmm . . . I don't know, Father," she said into the receiver, her eyes narrowing. "Putting her on a respirator . . . Who's recommending that anyway?" There was a pause. "But he *is* a specialist, right? You don't want some small-town GP in a situation like this." Another pause. "Did you hear anything from Marta yet? . . . How on earth can it take an entire day for her to get to a phone? Anyway, we can talk about that later. Nicole is here—finally—so we'll leave for the hospital right away and try to help you figure things out when we get there."

She hung up the phone and turned to face her daughter. "Well, Nicole, I specifically told you to meet us here at noon, didn't I?"

"It's only quarter after."

"Oh, lay off, Rachel," her husband snapped from the porch doorway where he now stood, sipping his steaming tea. "You always have to be hounding somebody."

"David," she began, straightening her frame to its full height, "stay out of—"

Nikki broke in before their argument went any further. "What about Gram? Dad said something else was wrong. What's going on?"

"Your grandmother's been put on a respirator. She's had some brain swelling from the clot, and this is standard procedure in such a case, the doctor said. I only hope he knows what he's doing." She stopped, eyeing Nikki intently up and down. "Nicole, you don't look well."

Great, here we go, Nikki thought. Had there ever been a time when her mother looked at her and said something positive?

"It's been only two days, but you actually look thinner than when you left home. Do you feel all right?"

Just great, Nikki thought. *As a matter of fact, I'm really getting into this throwing up every morning.*

"I should think you'd be pleased, Rachel," her father said from his place at the door. "You're always after her to lose weight."

"In the hips, David, not the face. See, she looks peaked in the face."

"Oh, come on," Nikki broke in before they could get warmed up. "I've been up half the night. How do you expect me to look? Now could we please just get to the hospital? Gram's probably back in her room by now, and it'll take 45 minutes to drive to Grand Rapids, so can we get going already? We're wasting time here." She picked up the overnight bag that she had filled with clothes and other things Grandpa had asked her to bring to the hospital. "We have to take those cakes, too, and drop them off at the library."

"Is everything else taken care of here?" Rachel Sheridan asked. "What about Gallie? Where is he anyway?"

"Probably back where he's been all night—lying in the doorway of Gram and Grandpa's bedroom. I think he's waiting for Gram to come home."

Nikki's mother frowned and started through the kitchen doorway to see for herself.

"He's not going to come to you, Mother. I had to put the leash on him just to get him outside this morning," Nikki called after her, but she disappeared into the living room.

"You know your mother. She'll have to go try for herself," Nikki's father said, setting his mug in the sink and clattering the spoon into it.

From the front hall, Rachel Sheridan's voice, coaxing, then insistent, floated back to them. "Gallie, come here, boy. . . . Come on, boy. . . . Would you get over here, dog!"

Nikki rolled her eyes and tapped her foot impatiently.

Mrs. Sheridan came back to the kitchen, shaking her head. She picked up her tapestry purse from the counter and stopped in front of the mirror on the wall by the back door. With deft fingers, she tucked two perfectly ordered strands of hair behind her left ear—just to make doubly sure they looked perfect—

then outlined her mouth precisely with a lipstick pencil. "That dog absolutely will not budge. I've never seen anything like it."

"Love, Rachel, love. It does marvelous things," Mr. Sheridan said. He picked up the cakes and pushed the kitchen door open with his elbow. "Can we please go now?"

Eight

IN GRAND RAPIDS, the sun was already breaking through the gray clouds, pulling a steamy, humid heat from the soggy ground. Nikki plucked at her shirt as they crossed the parking lot, struggling to unstick the damp material from between her shoulder blades.

Inside the hospital, any sensation of heat or humidity melted away. The air hung absolutely still, a stale, antiseptic smell suspended through the halls. *Just like the clinic*, Nikki thought.

She hurried across the lobby behind her parents. Part of her was terribly anxious to see Gram, to be with her and Grandpa, but another part boiled over with frustration as she followed her parents down the hall and into the elevator.

This whole abortion thing was supposed to be over with, finished, taken care of, by today. Leave it to me to forget about the Fourth. But then I couldn't have gone today anyway—not with my parents here. She felt like a mouse in a trap. *I won't be able to get away from these two all day, and I'll have to ride back to the house with them tonight, not to mention having to listen to their constant squabbling.*

A sign hung on the door of room 483: "Only Two Visitors At a Time, Please." But Mr. Sheridan strode in without hesitating. Nikki started to follow, then stopped short in the doorway.

Gram lay like a statue in a white bed with metal rails, her skin the color of paper. Grandpa sat on a chair pulled close beside the bed, hunched over her hand, stroking it gently with his own wrinkled one. It seemed the hand he held was the only part of her that wasn't attached to something. Her other hand was taped to a white plastic board, and an IV line, dangling from a plastic bag of clear solution, disappeared under the tape into her skin. A long, gray tube protruded from her mouth. Nikki shuddered, trying not to think how far down her throat the tube went.

Bulky machines crowded against the head of the bed, and the room was alive with their mechanical breathing. One must be a heart monitor, that much she could figure out. It emitted a steady *beep . . . beep . . . beep* in time with the pulsing green line on the screen. The other machine, the one that whirred and wheezed, must be a respirator, Nikki thought.

And in the middle of all the noise, her grandparents formed a kind of still life. Nikki found herself hanging back, reluctant to intrude.

David Sheridan cleared his throat, and Grandpa looked up. His face was gray with exhaustion and something more Nikki could hardly name. But he smiled and laid Gram's hand gently on the white sheet, taking care to place the fingers so they lay naturally on the bed. As she watched him, Nikki again saw in her mind the baby gulls covered with oil, the instinctive gentleness of his fingers cleaning their fragile legs.

Grandpa got to his feet stiffly, wincing a little as he straightened his knees, and reached out both arms to his daughter.

"Rachel, David, thank you for getting here so fast." He extended a hand to his son-in-law, keeping Nikki's mother close with his other arm. "I know it wasn't easy to get away."

Nikki watched her parents closely and heard a thought articulate itself in her mind, something she had only mutely understood before. *They always act better around Grandpa. They stop their incessant bickering and become almost . . . normal.*

"Here, Rachel, take my chair." Grandpa patted the plastic, turquoise cushions. "I'll pull up another one."

Grandpa came to Nikki then and put his arms around her tightly. She lay her head on his chest and felt the tears start to run down her cheeks against his wrinkled shirt.

"I want you to know—" he spoke over her head to her parents "—that Nikki did a great job last night. She got the ambulance there and Dr. Allen—I couldn't even think straight with Carole in such a condition, and Nikki took care of it all." He gave her an extra hug.

"How is she, Grandpa?" Nikki asked, her voice barely a whisper, looking back at the unmoving figure in the bed.

"Well, she's pretty much holding her own. There was some brain swelling, like I told your mother on the phone, but that seems to be subsiding. They did a spinal tap and the fluid's clear, and that's good news according to Carl, who's been explaining things to me all night. He says it means there's no hemorrhaging. We should get the results from the arteriogram later this afternoon."

"What's an arteriogram?" Nikki asked.

"It's a study of the blood vessels in the brain. They inject something into them that can be tracked on X-ray, and the images they get of the brain while this substance is passing through give a very clear picture of the blood vessels there. They have to find out exactly where in the brain the blood clot is, in case they have to go in after it."

"You mean, operate on her brain?" Nikki cried.

"Don't get upset yet, Nikki. That's just one possibility."

"Then you'll pretty much know what kind of damage to expect, right?" Mr. Sheridan asked, steering the conversation back to Gram's condition.

"As much as possible."

Nikki's mother, her elbows on the arms of the turquoise-colored chair, leaned her head into her hands and began to sob. Mr. Sheridan watched her closely, and a muscle in his jaw began to twitch.

Nikki stared. This was a side of her mother she'd never seen. Rachel Sheridan could slice you to ribbons with her words or wither you with a look, but she never, ever lost control.

"I can't stand this!" Mrs. Sheridan burst out when she finally raised her head. "What if she wakes up and she's crippled, or can't speak, or can't . . . can't even think? What will we do then?"

The room went still. Then, into the silence, Grandpa answered quietly, "We'll love her, Rachel, just like always."

She waved his words away with one hand. "You're so . . . you're so . . . naive! I don't think you have any idea how bad things can get. She may never wake up at all. Or she could wake up an absolute . . . vegetable."

"Stop it!" Grandpa said. Nikki had never heard her grandfather's voice so sharp. His face darkened and his tone was low, intense. "May I remind you that there are hundreds of documented cases of people in comas who heard every word spoken in their presence. Don't ever use that word again in front of your mother."

Nikki glanced from one face to the other, then got to her

feet and left the room. She couldn't stand any more of this tension. She strode back down the hall, her fists clenched. Leave it to her mother to get Grandpa all upset five minutes after she walked through the door! Rachel Sheridan never thought about how her words hurt other people.

As Nikki neared the corner, the elevator door slid open and there stood Marlene Allen and Carly, with Jeff behind. Jeff grinned at her from under his fishing hat and waggled his fingers in a small wave. Carly wore another Cubs T-shirt, and her short blond hair was pulled back with a leather headband.

"Nikki," Mrs. Allen asked, "how are you holding up? How's Carole? Any change?"

"She's the same. And I'm okay, I guess. Mother and Grandpa were having a . . . discussion . . . so I thought I'd go get something to drink. I didn't know you all were coming in this afternoon."

"Dad called and asked us to bring the car," Jeff answered. "He didn't have a way to get home, since he rode in the ambulance last night."

"And we wanted to see Carole, anyway," Mrs. Allen put in.

"We brought your grandpa's car, too, so he can drive home whenever he's ready," Jeff continued.

"Why don't I go on down to the room and see your parents, Nikki, and Carly and Jeff can go with you to get something to drink. The nurses won't want all of us in there at once anyway." She turned to Carly and Jeff. "I suppose you two are penniless, as usual."

Carly stuck out a ready hand. "Hey, if you're offering . . ."

Mrs. Allen laughed. She pulled some bills from her wallet and passed them to her daughter. Nikki couldn't help but notice, as they faced each other, how like mirror images they were—

the shining blond hair, the confident way they held themselves. Jeff, on the other hand, his dark hair falling across his forehead, seemed uncertain what to do with his newfound height and sometimes slouched a little in self-defense. But his smile was just like his mother's—kind, with a warmth that showed through from inside.

Nikki got into the elevator with Jeff and Carly, and the door slid shut.

"So if you're all here, what are the twins doing?"

"Nothing, we hope," Carly answered, laughing. She pushed the button for the first floor. "Mom thought they'd be okay alone for a little while."

"And we think she's nuts," Jeff said. "We'll probably find them out on the boat in the middle of the lake when we get home."

"Or on the roof," Carly added. The elevator stopped at the first floor, and the three stepped out and headed toward the hospital snack shop. "You should have seen it, Nik. Last spring, Mom left them alone for maybe 20 minutes, you know? And when we got home, they really were on the roof."

"Doing what?"

"Trying to catch a raccoon that had crawled down our chimney," Carly said. "Every time we leave those two alone, something happens. You can count on it."

"In fact," Jeff said as they slid into an empty booth, "I'm taking bets on whether or not they can stay out of trouble till we get home." He pulled a dollar bill out of his shorts pocket and laid it on the table in front of Carly.

"Are you kidding?" she asked. "I'm not throwing away good money. Abby and Adam are magnets for trouble."

"Listen to who's talking—after all the stunts you pulled when we were growing up!" Nikki said.

Carly put one hand on her hip and looked at Nikki indignantly. "Hey, those were all Jeff's ideas. I just did what he said."

"Oh, right, we all believe that," Jeff said. He stood up. "What would you like, Nik? I'll get the food for us."

They decided on Cokes and an order of fries to share, then Nikki remembered she hadn't eaten lunch, so she asked for a salad, too.

As soon as Jeff walked away, Carly leaned forward across the table.

"You know, Nik, you better watch out for my tall, dark, idiot brother."

"What?" Nikki burst out laughing again. Carly could always make her laugh, no matter how bad things were.

"No, listen, I'm serious. He was really worried about you yesterday—you know, when you were throwing up and all. He was asking Dad about your flu at dinner last night, like how long would it last and stuff."

"So what? That doesn't mean anything."

"Oh, yeah? Then he volunteered to come get you this morning for breakfast," Carly said, and then her face grew serious. "He feels really bad about your grandma—actually, we both do."

"Thanks, Carly. I just want everything to get back to normal, you know? Gram and Grandpa, you and Jeff and me . . ." *Especially me.* "I miss the three of us hanging around together, like last night on the pier. It doesn't feel like that was just last night, does it? So much has happened."

"Well," Carly added, "just don't forget what I said about Jeff. I've known him for 15 years now, so I can read the signs."

Jeff came back to the booth, carrying a red and white paper

boat heaped with golden fries, the steam still curling upward in wisps. He shoved a Coke across the table to Carly and handed Nikki her salad, along with four packets of dressing.

"You didn't say what kind you wanted, so I got you one of each."

Carly raised her eyebrows at Nikki, with an exaggerated sidelong glance at her brother.

"What?" he asked, looking back and forth at both of them.

"Oh, nothing." Carly grinned.

"Just ignore her, would you?" Nikki put in quickly, and when Jeff looked away, she frowned and shook her head at Carly.

Jeff ripped open several packets of ketchup and squeezed them onto an empty plate.

"You sure you have enough there, Jeff?" Carly teased, eyeing the mound of ketchup.

"Maybe it'll keep you busy dipping fries so Nikki and I can talk for a change," he answered. He took a fry and pushed it through the red mound until it was covered with ketchup. "So, Nik, what's going on with your grandma?"

"They're waiting for the results of a test called an arteriogram. The doctor's coming in this afternoon to tell us what they find."

"So they're looking to see what part of the brain's been damaged by the clot, right?" Jeff said.

"How'd you know that? I had to get Grandpa to explain all this." She blew the end of the wrapper off her straw.

"Dad's a doctor, remember? This kind of stuff is dinner conversation at our house."

"Grandpa says he's been a real help, explaining the tests and all. We sure were glad he was right next door last night."

Nikki ate her salad but left the fries for Jeff and Carly. The warm, oily smell of them made her stomach ache with hunger yet warned her off. When they finished eating, she sat back against the red-cushioned bench.

"I don't think we ought to go back to the room yet. Things weren't going real well with my mother and Grandpa when I left."

"You want to take a walk downtown?" Jeff asked. "It's just a couple of blocks."

"Well, I don't want to go too far," Nikki answered. "I know that sounds silly, but . . ."

"I know what," Carly broke in. "Let's go see the babies."

"What babies?" Nikki asked.

"In the nursery, of course. They're so cute."

"Oh, brother." Jeff rolled his eyes. "You always want to do that."

"Naturally. It's a girl thing, you know? Inborn sex differences. Hormones. Dad used to take us to see them all the time back in Chicago."

"Yeah," Jeff said, "when we were knee high and used to tag along on rounds with him."

"So what? I liked it. And you did, too, before you turned into such a big macho man." She batted her lashes at him.

Jeff grinned, his ears red along the rims. "Okay, okay, I liked it. I admit it. So let's go. There's nothing else to do here."

The directory in the lobby listed obstetrics on the fifth floor. As soon as they stepped off the elevator, Nikki knew she'd made a mistake. Pictures of mothers and babies shot in a soft, fuzzy focus lined the light-coral walls.

Signs pointed the way toward the nursery at the end of the hall. One part of Nikki wanted to turn and run back to the elevator. *Oh, right. Wouldn't that look good in front of Jeff and Carly?* But another part of her felt an undeniable pull to see the babies behind those windows.

Three bassinets were pushed up close to the nursery windows so admiring family members could see. Each baby was wrapped snugly in a blue-and-pink striped blanket, allowing only little heads to show. Two of the babies were sleeping soundly, their only movements an occasional shudder. The third cried wildly, his eyes squeezed shut, his face dark-red from . . . what? Hunger? Anger? What did babies that tiny feel, anyway?

"Why's he screaming like that?" Nikki asked. "You think he's hungry?"

"Of course," Carly said. "Don't you ever baby-sit? They're always hungry."

"I baby-sit, sure, but not for newborns like this."

"He could just be lonely," Jeff said, staring down at the furious child. "Stuck in the nursery like that."

There were other windows, farther down the hall. Nikki walked to them, curious, and looked inside. It was another nursery, but this one was crowded with machines covered with all kinds of dials and tubes. At first, she thought the room was unused, then she saw the lone baby lying in a glass box. Tubes from one of the machines were connected to the box, and the dials were flickering slightly.

The infant was so small that Nikki almost missed it. *It's like a skinny miniature version of the other babies*, she thought. She stared at the minute fingers and toes, the knobby knees hardly bigger than one of her knuckles. A light-blue knit hat, like the ones children wore to go sledding in the winter, circled its tiny skull. From underneath the hat, lead wires ran to a second machine. Carly and Jeff walked up behind her.

"Look at this one," Nikki whispered. "He's hardly as long as my foot!"

"Yeah, this is the preemie nursery," Carly explained. "See all those machines? When babies are born this early, their lungs aren't completely developed yet, so they need a lot of help to make it."

A nurse noticed them then, and she crossed the nursery to pull the curtains shut.

"Nice lady," Nikki said.

"They don't really like people staring at the preemies," Jeff said. "Lots of times the parents come in and sit by their babies, so the nurses try to give them some privacy."

They started back toward the elevator.

"How early can a baby be born and be all right?" Nikki asked.

"Dad says it's down to about 24 weeks now," Jeff answered. "It's always changing, though, because doctors keep learning new ways to take care of them. A few years ago, babies born that early didn't have a chance, but lots of them survive now."

"Oooh, listen to the next medical genius!" Carly teased, then caught herself as she tripped on the edge of the elevator door.

Jeff crossed his arms over his chest and leaned against the back wall of the elevator. "You walk much?" he asked her.

Nikki couldn't help but laugh. For once, Carly was left without a comeback.

The door slid shut and the elevator started downward.

"Do you really want to be a doctor, Jeff?" Nikki asked.

"I'm thinking about it. I'll see how my grades turn out this year."

He went on, but Nikki didn't hear the rest. She couldn't get rid of the picture in her mind of that tiny infant with the woolly blue hat.

Nine

WHEN THEY STEPPED off the elevator on the fourth floor, Nikki was relieved to see her parents and grandfather talking calmly with Marlene Allen in the hall outside Gram's room. Maybe Mrs. Allen's arrival had helped. She and Nikki's mother had been friends for years.

"We're about ready to go," Mrs. Allen said to Jeff and Carly as they approached. "Your dad's still sound asleep in the waiting room. I haven't had the heart to wake him up yet, but I guess I'd better."

"He's been asleep since 9:30." Nikki's grandfather shook his head in wonder. "I don't know how he does it. I couldn't do more than catnap on that vinyl couch."

"Long years of training, that's how," Mrs. Allen said with a laugh. "In residency, you learn to sleep anywhere, anytime, or you don't survive. In fact, that's how Carl refers to residency—Sleep Deprivation 101." She turned to Nikki's parents. "Well, we're headed back to the lake. Anything we can do, just let us know." She hugged Nikki's mother good-bye. "We'll make sure Gallie gets out when you're not around, and I'll water Carole's flowers. And we're praying all the time. You know that."

The hall seemed deserted once the Allens turned the corner.

"It's pretty late. Would you like to get some lunch in the snack shop?" Grandpa asked.

"I just ate some stuff with Jeff and Carly," Nikki answered. "You all go ahead. I'll stay here with Gram."

Except for the mechanical beeps and whirrings, Gram's room was quiet. After a few minutes, even the electronic noises faded into the background. Gram lay exactly as she had an hour before. Even her right hand was just where Grandpa had placed it on the bed.

Nikki turned away and picked up a copy of *Time* magazine someone had left in the room. She leafed through it and tried to read an article about Madonna but couldn't make any sense of the words. Gram's presence was too strong.

Nikki felt sick and awkward when she looked at her grandmother but uneasy when she looked away, as though Gram might feel ignored. Finally, she gave up, dropped the magazine back on the table, and went to sit in the turquoise chair beside the bed.

"Gram," she began. "Gram?" She reached out tentatively and touched that still right hand, patting it gently. The skin was warm to the touch and dry. "I know it's crazy to try to talk to you, but . . . well, I just want you to know I'm so sorry about . . . this whole thing. Happening to you, I mean."

Nikki glanced back over her shoulder, then got up and pushed the thick wooden door shut. It closed slowly against the doorpost and finally latched with a heavy click. She went back to the bed.

"We all feel really bad," she tried again. "I hope you're not in pain or anything." She sat, silent, for a few minutes, trying to think of something else to say.

"Gallie won't leave your bedroom, Gram. Ever since last night, he just lies in the doorway, waiting for you, I guess. He won't eat or anything."

Nikki stopped, then added quickly, "But I put his food and water dishes right there beside him, so he can get to them whenever he wants. And I made him go out for a walk with me. He didn't want to, but I used the leash." Nikki watched her grandmother closely. There was no twitch, no flicker of response.

"This is crazy. You can't hear a single thing I say, can you? Oh, Gram, where are you?"

Nikki cried a little then, partly from the sadness of it, partly for herself. Then, hardly aware of what she was doing, she found she couldn't keep her secret anymore.

"Gram, I can't talk to anybody else in the whole world about this. Please come back. I really need you. . . ." She stopped to wipe away the tears spilling down her cheeks. "Gram, listen. I'm pregnant. And I don't know what to do. I didn't mean for it to happen. I just liked T.J. so much—for two years I liked him—and he turned out to be such a jerk. I thought he cared about me, too, or I never would have let him. It's my own fault, I know. But now I don't know what to do."

She stopped, stroking her grandmother's hand gently. She looked at the fingers, thickened a little from years of gardening and kitchen work. Or maybe from all those years of workouts at the piano.

A faint pulse beat steadily in the knobby veins crisscrossing the back of Gram's hand, in perfect time with the *beep, beep, beep* of the heart monitor. Unaccountably, Nikki felt better. After a few minutes, she spoke again.

"Thanks anyway, Gram. I know you'd listen if you could. I guess I just have to solve this one myself, like Mother's always telling me."

She reached up and brushed a strand of gray hair back from her grandmother's forehead. Gram would be upset if she could see the way her hair looked now, but Nikki was afraid to do more, for fear of jarring one of the tubes or needles. Just as Grandpa had, she lay Gram's limp hand back on the bed sheet, carefully positioning it so it looked comfortable.

Nikki thought the end of the day would never come. She sat with her parents and Grandpa beside Gram's bed, making uneasy small talk. She paced up and down the hall, trying to avoid looking into the open doors of other rooms. She went to the vending machine and got snacks for everyone, and she spent a long time staring out the window at the city below.

The only magazines she could find in the waiting room were all old, their covers ripped, the corners of the pages curled over. She changed positions in the stiff chairs a hundred times, trying to find some comfortable way to sit, and finally gave up.

She stretched out on the couch in the empty waiting room and was just drifting off to sleep when an entire family walked in. She jumped up off the couch, embarrassed, though she didn't know why, and went back to pacing the hall.

The most exciting thing that happened all day was Aunt Marta's phone call from the Dominican Republic, and Nikki missed even that, since she was downstairs in the snack shop again when it came through.

"Will she get here soon?" Nikki demanded when she heard about it.

"Next week," Grandpa answered.

"Next week! Why isn't she coming right away?"

"Because the class she's teaching only lasts another week, and people are there from all over the island. If she leaves, there's no one else to teach. And with your grandma in a coma, all Marta could do is sit here like the rest of us." For just a moment, there was a bleakness in his eyes, then he went on. "So I told her to wait until the class is done and then come."

Nikki turned and left the room quickly, swallowing hard to hold back her disappointment.

Later that evening, as she turned to make another circuit down the hall, the elevator doors opened. There stood Jeff, for the second time that day. Nikki couldn't keep from grinning. Even his fishing hat looked good to her.

"What are you doing here?" she burst out. "It's nine o'clock!"

"I know." He grinned, his dark eyes crinkling at the corners. "I also know it's the Fourth of July, and we had plans to see the fireworks, remember? From the boat, I know, but since we can't do that, I thought you might like to watch them with me here in Grand Rapids. What do you say?"

"Anywhere!" she said. "Just get me out of here. My parents want to stay late in case something happens, but I don't see what good we're doing. Gram doesn't have a clue that we're here."

"Well, come on then, let's go."

Nikki smoothed her hair back with both hands, suddenly aware that she hadn't looked in a mirror for several hours.

"You're really serious, aren't you?" she asked him.

"Look, lady, I didn't drive all the way into town just to entertain you with jokes. I think you need a break. Here, look." He pulled a wrinkled flyer from the pocket of his khaki shorts. "'Riverside concert in the park, 8:00 to 9:30,'" he read. "'Breathtaking fireworks display over the Grand River at 9:45.' You wouldn't want to miss a *breathtaking* fireworks display, would you?" He stopped and looked at her, his eyebrows raised in question.

"All right, all right, I'll go!" she laughed. "Just let me tell my parents what we're doing."

"Too late. I already took care of that when I met them in the lobby. They were going for another cup of coffee, the fifty-seventh one today, according to your dad."

"And they don't mind me leaving?"

"Nope. They didn't act like it."

"What about your folks? And Carly and the twins?"

"They took the boat out and followed the original plan."

"Do they mind you not going with them?"

"Nah, it's fine. They all think you need a break, too. I would've brought Carly, but she hates the noise downtown—it can be pretty overwhelming when the fireworks start booming and the sound ricochets off the buildings. We came once when Carly was little, and it nearly scared the pants off her."

"Well, come with me, and I'll say good-bye to Grandpa, and to Gram." They walked together back down the hall to the room.

Grandpa sat as he had earlier in the day, close by the bedside. One of the books Nikki had brought from home lay open on his lap, and he read aloud from it so Gram could hear, glancing at her face now and then as he said the words.

Nikki wrapped her arms around his shoulders from behind and leaned over to kiss his cheek, which was bristled now with gray whiskers over his soft, tanned skin. He squeezed her hands tightly while he finished the sentence, then looked up at her with a smile.

"Grandpa, Jeff wants me to go downtown to see the fireworks. Would you mind?"

"Not at all, honey. You've put in a long, long day here. Your parents want to stay for a while yet, and I'm going to spend the night again."

"Oh, Grandpa, don't you think you ought to come home and get some rest? You could ride back with Jeff and me."

"Don't worry, I'll rest," he said, patting her hand. "There's only one place I want to be when your grandma wakes up, and that's right here. You two hurry up. It gets really crowded downtown on the Fourth. You'll want to find a good spot to see the show."

In the elevator, Nikki spoke her thoughts aloud. "Jeff, do you think he's just dreaming? Or do you think she could really come out of this coma?"

"Sure she could," Jeff said. "I've heard of lots of people who wake up from comas. I don't see any reason your grandmother couldn't be one of them."

A few moments later, the elevator doors opened, and they made their way across the deserted lobby. Jeff pushed the hospital door open, and they walked out onto the street. It was a shock to trade the climate-controlled, sterile atmosphere of the hospital for the steamy summer evening outside. In the hot, humid air, it didn't take long for Nikki's hair to weigh heavily on the back of her neck. The jeans she had put on in the cool, rainy morning now felt stiff and awkward as she and Jeff hurried down the steep hill into the city.

Everywhere, people milled about. Adults led small children from the parking garages toward the riverside park, carrying blankets and lawn chairs. The sky was just beginning to darken above the shallow hills around the edge of the city. In the west, the orange glow of sunset still lit the sky brightly, with long, thin strips of purple clouds lying low on the horizon.

"Jeff, smell the hot dogs? And popcorn! I am so hungry."

He laughed. "Come on. Let's get closer, down by the river, then I'll find you some food, okay?" But his voice was drowned out by an orchestra, which had struck up a Sousa march.

"What? What'd you say?" Nikki hurried to keep up. She sidestepped two little boys who stood on the curb, clad only in shorts, swinging their hissing sparklers in wild arcs. Their arms flailed madly, and their smooth, tan skin rippled up and down over their ribs like thin silk on a washboard as the sparklers etched bright multicolored circles in the air.

"I said . . ." Jeff tried to repeat himself, but gave up when he saw she couldn't hear. Finally, he put his face down to the side of her head and repeated his words into her hair, his warm breath tickling her neck and ear. She nodded, and they kept going, squeezing between groups of people packed shoulder to shoulder in front of the band shell. The warm, meaty smell from the yellow hot dog carts made Nikki's hollow stomach ache.

"'Scuse me, 'scuse me," Nikki said, trying to push through the crowd, but it was useless. She ended up simply elbowing her way after Jeff's white T-shirt-clad back. At last, they broke out of the densest part of the crowd and walked a little way downstream on a paved path along the riverbank. There was less noise here, and they found they could talk again.

"What a madhouse, huh?" Jeff laughed. "It's nuts, but they do great fireworks here."

"I don't care how crazy it is. Anything's better than the hospital. It was so quiet in there I thought I'd lose my mind."

"Ah-hah! So you *were* glad to see me!" Jeff looked at her from under the rim of the fishing hat, his blue eyes crinkled nearly shut in a grin.

"Well, yeah, sure I was. I would've been glad to see any-body. Why?"

"Oh, I don't know." He shrugged. "I just wasn't sure this was such a brilliant idea."

"What do you mean?"

"Trying to get you to leave your grandmother and all. But I figured you were probably feeling pretty cooped up."

"Actually, I do feel kind of guilty about being out here enjoy-ing myself. It wasn't like I was helping Gram any by just sitting there, though, so I guess it doesn't matter, right?" Before Jeff could answer, Nikki pointed to another hot dog vendor set up at the foot of one of the bridges and said, "Look!"

He laughed. "Still dying of hunger, huh? Come on, we'll get something before the show starts." They picked their way through groups of people on blankets and lawn chairs.

"You want the works?" Jeff asked, as a small, dark-eyed man beside the cart smoked patiently, waiting for their order. "He has chili dogs and . . . let's see." He scanned the menu board hung with metal rings on the front of the cart. "You can have cheese and onions and hot peppers . . ."

"No, no, that's okay." Nikki stopped him quickly. The sudden churning in her stomach added to the aching hunger was not a pleasant sensation. "Just plain, with ketchup."

While they waited for the food, they watched more and more people crowd onto the lighted bridges.

"You know, Nik, I didn't think of it before, but I bet that's the best place to be—out there over the water. You want to see if we can find a place on the bridge?" He paid the man, then zigzagged thin lines of ketchup down each side of the sizzling hot dog.

"Fine with me," Nikki agreed, biting into the soft bun and the hot, salty meat inside.

They fought their way out to the middle of the bridge and found a place to sit on the iron railing. Next to them was a family with three small, squirming children in summer pajamas. The youngest, a blue-eyed girl with long, curly blond hair pulled back in a ponytail, was already starting to cry in a fretful, tired-sounding whine. Jeff and Nikki glanced at each other, and Jeff rolled his eyes. But then the first tentative pops sounded in the sky above them, and even the blond child's crying quieted.

The sky had faded to a pale mauve in the west. Directly above the city, it showed blue-black as darkness took over. From far up the river, the orchestra played the last strains of the "1812 Overture" and Nikki could feel the vibrations of the cannon shots in the bridge beneath her feet.

Jeff leaned over and whispered to her, "They must play that thing all over the country on the Fourth."

Nikki was aware of the warm, wheaty smell of his tanned skin, but she only nodded, laughing.

Then, into the still, dark sky, there burst an explosion of color. A huge umbrella of white opened directly over their heads, and as the hot light fell from the sky, it turned to emerald green and brilliant red. Nikki glanced down at the river and saw the umbrella reversed, reflected in the water. For an instant, they were surrounded with color, but before she could marvel at it, another explosion boomed, echoing off the high buildings lining the river, and the lights fell again in slow motion into the darkness, fading as they fell.

The little blond girl started to cry in earnest now, burying her face in her mother's shoulder. The older children, a boy and girl, clung to their father's legs, wide-eyed.

"I hope they don't make those kids stay," Jeff whispered. "This is what scared Carly so bad when she was little."

The parents tried to reason with the children, but the tiny girl's cries turned to wails. Then her brother and sister started to sniffle. Finally, the parents gave up and started to work their way back through the crowd toward the shore as the next lights burst overhead.

This time they were encircled in brilliant bright-blue, and Nikki watched, entranced, as once again the lights fell around them and seemed to rise from the water at the same time. From thousands of voices up and down the riverbank came the standard Fourth of July chant: "Oooh, aaaah." But Nikki was silent, too caught up in the beauty to make a sound.

"You like your hot dogs cold, huh?" Jeff asked her, nodding at the half-eaten food in her hand.

"I forgot all about it," she said with a laugh, then took another bite.

"Sounds like a whole new diet strategy to me—distraction therapy. Maybe I'll be one of those diet doctors and really rake in the dough."

Nikki waited for the next explosion to die down. "Are you saying I need to go on a diet, Jeff Allen?"

He turned and looked at her in the red light reflected from the sky, and his gaze was steady. "No, Nikki. You look fine to me just the way you are."

Nikki was glad for the loud boom that reverberated then. She ate the rest of her hot dog in silence. The display went on and on, but after a few more explosions, her thoughts slipped back to Gram, lying in her hospital room, deaf and blind to this whole display. And, hard as she tried, she couldn't keep from thinking about herself. It was foolish to worry yet—how could anyone know?—but each day that passed without getting the abortion made her more and more uneasy.

What if she threw up in front of everyone again? People weren't stupid—a two-year-old could figure out her secret if she did that. And then another thought came, one she hadn't thought of before: What if she had a miscarriage and had to go to the hospital? She winced at the thought, then was startled when Jeff spoke.

"Looks like the grand finale."

Suddenly, light saturated the night sky. The tempo of the booms turned insistent, relentless. Standing out on the bridge over the water, the effect was overwhelming. *It's a good thing they got those kids out of here*, Nikki thought.

Thousands of "oohs" and "aahs" mixed with clapping and whistling, then the last lights faded to darkness. Throngs of people started back toward the parking garages and side streets. Jeff and Nikki stayed on the bridge, watching.

"You in a hurry?" Jeff asked. "There's going to be a monster traffic jam for miles, no matter which way we try to go."

Nikki picked at the peeling flakes of lime-green paint on the metal railing where they sat. "You either have to leave really early, like those people who always duck out during the last number at a concert, or be patient, I guess."

"Or get caught in the middle of traffic going five miles an hour."

"No thanks. I'd rather wait," Nikki said.

At first, the bridge trembled under the footfalls of so many people, but gradually the crowds thinned out. Soon it grew quiet enough that Nikki could hear Jeff whistling softly under his breath. The water gurgled as it tumbled against the bridge pilings beneath them, smelling faintly of fish. The air was heavy with moisture now, and Nikki shivered slightly at its touch against her arms.

They talked for a while about school, about Jeff's plans for his senior year. Nikki relaxed, starting to feel sleepy as they spoke.

"Nikki?" Jeff stood up and turned, leaning over the railing to look into the dark, bubbling water below.

"Yeah?"

"Are you doing okay with all this—your grandma, I mean?"

"I guess so. It happened so fast that there wasn't time to think until today. Then, at the hospital, none of it even seemed real to me. I mean, how can a person be perfectly normal, baking cakes and stuff one day, then be lying in a hospital bed, totally out of it, the next? It just happened too fast. I feel like I haven't caught up yet."

And if you only knew, she thought. *That's not the half of it.*

"What about the flu?" he asked. "You think you're over it?"

Something in his voice made her look in his direction before she answered. "Yeah, I think so. I feel fine now."

They were quiet for a minute, and Nikki saw that the moon was dimly visible again over the city lights.

"Nik, can I ask you something?" He didn't wait for a reply. "What was really bothering you yesterday at Rosie's?"

She stalled, sliding down from the railing and brushing paint chips off the back of her jeans deliberately before she answered. "Just what I told you. Come on, Jeff, let's go." She started for the end of the bridge. "I'm so tired I can hardly keep my eyes open."

As they climbed back uphill, Nikki walked just quickly enough to make talking difficult, and Jeff didn't probe any further. Once they reached the red Bronco in the hospital parking garage, she pretended she was too tired to talk. And somewhere, on the long drive home, she really did fall asleep, curled up in the front seat beside Jeff.

✤ Ten ✤

THE NEXT FEW DAYS blurred together like the view from a rushing roller coaster. Nikki's parents expected her to go into the hospital each day with them, so while Jeff and Carly spent their time at the beach, Nikki sat through long, silent days in Gram's dimly lit hospital room, punctuated by daily treks back and forth between Rosendale and Grand Rapids on the glaring, hot expressway.

In between there was laundry to do and meals to fix and beds to be made. And always, building inside her was the panic that someone would figure it out—the weight loss, the throwing up, the dark circles under her eyes. There was never a time when she could get away, when she could get back to the clinic to do what had to be done.

The nights were strange and hot, filled with troubling dreams that she could never quite recount when daylight finally came. Except for one. She woke up in the morning with every detail vivid in her mind.

In that dream, Nikki stood in front of a school assembly,

calm and confident, with no trace of the shyness that usually kept her on the fringes in real life. Everyone was clapping wildly for her, and she had the impression she'd just made some incredibly witty remark. Mr. Anderson, Millbrook High's balding, treble-voiced principal, mounted the steps to the stage, carrying something that he held out to Nikki. Some sort of award, she supposed. But when she took the bundle from him, she saw it was an infant, wrapped in a blue-and-pink striped blanket, his tiny, downy head covered with a blue knit hat.

Things moved faster after that. Somehow, then, T.J. was beside her on the stage, and she held up the baby for him to see. A look of tenderness crossed his face, and he put one arm around her, the other around the child. The feeling of love was so warm, so palpable, that she had the sensation of leaning back into it.

Then, from far back in the audience, someone laughed, just one little twitter, but it rippled throughout the auditorium. Soon the whole student body was laughing. T.J.'s expression turned to disgust. He strode off the platform, and suddenly Lauren was there, laughing like everyone else. T.J. put his arm around her, and they disappeared into the crowd.

The hurt inside was so great that Nikki woke herself up with deliberate effort. She started to rub her eyes and found her face soaked with tears. The feeling of the dream depressed her all that day.

At the hospital, things weren't much better. Nikki watched, helpless, as Grandpa tried to lure back the woman he loved from wherever it was she was wandering, out of his reach. He spent each night on a cot in her room. And each day, he called Nikki to bring something else to the hospital, some other book or tape, that might urge Gram to awaken. He read aloud from the books Nikki had already taken in, he read chapters of the Bible that Gram especially loved, and he talked for hours every day, reminding her of memories that only the two of them shared.

Once, Nikki blundered into the room and overheard him, then backed away on tiptoe. She felt as though she had interrupted him at his prayers.

When he couldn't talk anymore, Grandpa turned on Gram's favorite tapes, everything from the Brandenburg Concertos to soundtracks of musicals she had collected over the years. By Grandpa's design, there was always something happening in room 483, something that would call Gram back, if she could hear anything at all. But no one knew if that was possible.

Her father left on Monday night to go home to Ohio. He said the judge refused to grant a continuance that would have allowed him more time away from his case. But Nikki could see he was glad to go. *Maybe the judge didn't say that at all. Dad probably made it up so he could get away from here.*

Rachel Sheridan wasn't happy. "Listen, I have to stay until I find out what's going to happen," she had told her husband. "So what exactly do you expect me to do without a car, David?"

"Don't be ridiculous, Rachel. You can use Nikki's car, of course."

And Nikki had fled upstairs to her room and slammed her fist hard into the feather pillow, over and over, because always, in the back of her mind, the pressure was mounting. She had been waiting for her parents to leave so they wouldn't be watching her every move. It had never occurred to her that her mother would stay on. How was she supposed to get to Howellsville now? Without a car? And with her mother breathing down her neck?

Nikki and her mother were left alone in the big, old house where Mrs. Sheridan had grown up. A few times, for about two seconds apiece, the thought flashed through Nikki's mind that maybe, just maybe, she might dare talk to her mother about the pregnancy. She had heard of cases when people changed suddenly in the face of a crisis. Maybe her mother—? Then her mind would clear. *I might as well run naked down Main Street as to tell her.*

She couldn't go on this way much longer, though. No matter what she ate—or even if she ate nothing at all—she threw up every morning. After that, the nausea usually subsided for the rest of the day. But vomiting was a noisy business. She flushed the toilet several times during each bathroom bout, trying to cover the sound, always worried her mother would hear.

For her part, Rachel Sheridan grew more impatient with the situation each day. She spent long hours on the phone with her theater friends back in Ohio, checking on the progress of rehearsals. In between phone calls, she sat at the big grand piano in the living room and practiced all the songs in her role, over and over. Even when Nikki felt like playing, which wasn't often these days, Mrs. Sheridan was always in the way.

On Wednesday morning, when Nikki came back from her daily walk with the dog, she heard voices in the kitchen. Gallie, who was still keeping a vigil for Gram, disappeared slowly up the stairs, and Nikki stopped dead in the front hall, listening.

"...cannot stand to see him like this much longer, Marlene," her mother was saying. "He's lost weight, he's so exhausted he can't think straight, but he won't give up. He won't even come home to rest."

"I know, Rachel, I know," Mrs. Allen said in reply. "But he's doing what he thinks is important."

"Look, Marlene, my mother has absolutely no idea that he's even there. All these tapes he's playing and books he's reading to her—she can't hear any of it. It's just wasted effort. Very noble, but wasted. Don't get me wrong. I feel just as bad about her as he does. I mean, she's my mother, for heaven's sake. But life has to go on. Even if she does wake up now, the doctor says she'll have terrible brain damage. If she lives, she'll probably spend the rest of her life in some rehab place."

"Sometimes," Mrs. Allen said slowly, and Nikki, who had moved down the hall, could see her stirring her tea, frowning a little as she always did when trying to get her thoughts together, "sometimes these coma cases surprise you, Rachel. I've heard Carl tell about people who made astounding recoveries. I mean, you wouldn't want to give up too soon."

"I don't believe in miracles, Marlene."

"I think what your father's trying to do is very special. His love for Carole is tremendously strong. He's just fighting to get her back the only way he knows how."

"That's a very idealistic way to look at it, Marlene. I just don't believe it works in the real world. I think I need to speak to him when I get there today, tell him it may be time to give up."

"I wish you wouldn't, Rachel, at least not yet. Hope is all he has right now. And faith."

"Faith!" Nikki's mother spit the word out. "A lot of good that will do."

Nikki bunched up Gallie's thin leash and shoved it into her

pocket as she whirled around and ran upstairs to her bedroom. She didn't want to hear any more.

Later that day, on the drive to the hospital, Mrs. Sheridan practiced her music.

"I always tell my students that being a vocalist has its advantages," she said. Nikki had heard that line so often she could have chimed in and made it a duet. "I can practice anywhere, unlike pianists, for instance, who are tied to a keyboard."

The old Rodgers and Hammerstein melodies from the show were pretty, though. *She really is good*, Nikki thought.

But she couldn't shake the misery that enveloped her each time she heard her mother sing. She leaned her head against the car window and shut her eyes. How old had she been when she first understood the truth she had grown up with, that nothing was more important to Rachel Sheridan than her music?

Not more than five years old, maybe not even that, because she'd had to stretch on tiptoe to see over the glossy black side of the grand piano in the family room. She knew the rules, but that day she'd crept closer anyway, fascinated with the sparkling notes, with the beauty her mother was creating. When the music ended, she had cried out in delight, "Sing it again, sing it again," clapping her hands.

Rachel had slammed her hand down on the keys in a discordant crash of fury. "Are you *ever* supposed to interrupt me when I'm practicing? *Ever?*"

The beauty shattered around Nikki. She had been too young to reconcile the mother that read her books and played Barbies one moment, then exploded in rage the next. Looking at the floor to escape those angry blue eyes, she shook her head slowly.

"How many times have I told you that? How am I ever supposed to learn this music with you bothering me all the time?"

Even looking back after all those years, Nikki still wondered
in amazement how a voice so beautiful could turn so harsh.

"Now go play and leave me alone while I'm working!" her
mother had scolded. But Rachel Sheridan was always working.

In the seat beside her now, Mrs. Sheridan switched back to
scales and arpeggios, moving up the scale in precisely measured
intervals, each vowel sound beautifully rounded and projected
directly ahead at the windshield.

At the hospital, Nikki hugged her grandfather gently because
his face was so white and strained. Then she settled back into the
hospital routine. She sat alone with Gram while Grandpa and
her mother went downstairs for lunch. The machines beeped
and whirred exactly as they had on her first visit, but today
Nikki didn't even try to talk. She just sat quietly, in a kind of
limbo, searching her imagination for some excuse to drive to
Howellsville for the abortion but unable to think of anything
good enough to convince her mother.

But in the back of her mind, a sense of uneasiness now surrounded her plans. What if—just suppose—it wasn't propaganda those demonstrators had handed her at the clinic?

Nikki shook her head, trying to erase the thought. She got
out of her chair and leaned against the windowsill. From here,
she could look down on most of the city. The walkways lining
the riverbank, even the bridge where she and Jeff had watched
fireworks, were all visible. She knew that somewhere in those
buildings was the museum where Grandpa had taken her and
Jeff and Carly. The one with the display about the babies. She

pulled the phone book from the drawer of Gram's bedside table and looked up the address.

~⁀

When Grandpa and her mother returned, Nikki was relieved to see them. "How was lunch?" she asked.

"About like you'd expect from a hospital cafeteria." Grandpa winked at her and lowered himself with a sigh onto the turquoise cushions of the bedside chair. He reached out and took his wife's limp hand in his own.

"We're back, Carole. You didn't miss much as far as lunch was concerned, sweetie, though I dare say you'd have traded your glucose IV for our hamburgers, right?" He rubbed his thumb gently over the blue vein on the back of her hand. "Listen, as soon as you wake up, I'll get you anything you want to eat."

Mrs. Sheridan sat in a chair across the bed from her father, her mouth a tight line, her eyes narrowed.

She's winding up, Nikki thought. *Any minute now he's going to get both barrels.*

But before she had a chance, Grandpa turned to face his granddaughter. "You know, I keep meaning to ask how you're feeling, Nikki, and with all that's been going on, I keep forgetting. I take it you're all over that flu bug by now."

Nikki went cold all over, but she tried to sound nonchalant. "I'm fine, Grandpa."

"Rachel, you wouldn't believe how sick this girl was that first morning after she got here, throwing up and all, white as a sheet, and I never even got to tell you. She said there was a lot of flu down in Millbrook before she left, that even you and David had a touch of it."

Mrs. Sheridan's eyes narrowed further, but this time she

fixed her shrewd, calculating gaze on her daughter. Nikki licked her lips, which had suddenly gone dry. Her heart started to pound, and she tried to take long, even breaths without being obvious.

Her mother's reply came slow and deliberate. "I can't really think what Nicole was talking about. I didn't hear of any flu going around, and David and I have been just fine."

Nikki turned back to the window. *Don't let her go on, please, please. Don't let Grandpa ask any more questions.*

As though in answer, a nurse bustled into the room, pulling a blood pressure cuff from her jacket pocket.

"Time for vitals again, folks," she said cheerily. "It'll just take a minute." She checked the drip rate on the IV bag against her watch, adjusted a knob ever so slightly, and checked again. Nikki saw her chance and walked to the door.

"I'm going for a Coke. Anybody want anything?"

"We just had lunch, dear," her mother answered, a little too sweetly.

Nikki turned and fled. Alone in the elevator, she leaned her head against the wall. *How can Grandpa be so stupid?* she thought, knowing all the while how unfair she was being. *She'll be all over me for an explanation the minute we get in the car. I'll just tell her . . . what? I'll tell her a lot of my friends had the flu, and that's all I meant.*

Nikki stayed in the snack shop as long as she could, but she knew they would wonder where she was if she didn't get back soon. As the elevator purred its way to the fourth floor, she tried to store up answers for any questions her mother might throw at her, but when she neared Gram's room, she realized she needn't have worried.

Her mother's voice, strident with anger, carried out into the hall. Nikki could tell by her words that the conversation had been going on for some time.

"Look, I just think it's ridiculous. You're so tired you can hardly sit up in your chair, but you keep this whole facade going day after day—the reading, the music, the talking. Why are you doing this? She can't hear a thing you say!"

Nikki stopped just outside the door, her arms folded across her chest, and leaned her head against the door frame.

"I'm doing it because I love her. Try to understand, Rachel. She's worth it to me."

"All I'm saying is that you need to face reality here. Look at her. She's not even aware of you, no matter what you want to think. She's not aware of anything. For all we know, if she does ever wake up, she may be so brain-damaged that she'll be a veg—"

"I told you never to say that again!" Grandpa thundered.

"Well, it's true! And somebody has to make you face it!"

"And if it is true, it won't change a thing," Grandpa answered.

"What do you mean?"

"There may well come a time when I have to face the fact that your mother has irreversible brain damage, that I'm not doing any good by trying to reach her. The doctors just don't know yet. But it won't change my love for her. Just because she can't give anything back to me doesn't mean she's no longer valuable to me." He paused, but she said nothing.

"Rachel, listen to me!" Grandpa continued. "Love is not about what makes you or me feel good—it's about being there when someone needs you. Sometimes that means self-sacrifice, remember? 'And we ought to lay down our lives for our brothers . . .'"

Nikki's mother gave an indignant snort. "Don't trot out

your Christianity in front of me. You know I never bought in to all of that, so there's no use quoting Bible verses at me. And I don't agree with all this self-sacrifice business. You can't let anyone demand that much of you."

"But Rachel, we can't live without other people sacrificing for us. And we can't live any kind of meaningful life without returning that sacrifice. No matter what you think of Christianity now, Rachel, there was a time when you understood that God put the whole cycle into motion with Jesus Christ and His death for us."

"I don't want to hear this," she snapped.

"I know. Ever since you ..."

"No! Stop it!"

Nikki looked at the gray carpet of the hallway and understood they were discussing far more than Gram's stroke. *They have two totally opposite views of life.*

Nikki realized, staring down at the carpet, that she had always just assumed she'd grow up like Gram and Grandpa. A better person than her mother. Or father. But there in the hospital hallway, she suddenly understood that Grandpa had become the man she loved so dearly by the choices he'd made.

But to be like him might mean—would probably mean—putting aside this whole idea of having an abortion. *And then I'd have to go through the whole pregnancy....*

She ran down all four flights of stairs, pushed open the glass doors of the hospital with both hands, and headed down the hill into the city. They'd never miss her.

By the time Nikki found the museum, her green rayon shirt was dark with sweat. Even her white shorts clung to her legs. She pushed her damp, wildly curling hair back off her face and wished for a barrette or rubber band, anything to get it out of the way.

When she stepped inside the museum, cold air enveloped her. She savored the touch of it for a moment and allowed her eyes to adjust from the blazing sun to the darkness of the nearly deserted building. Then she began to search.

Her footsteps echoed hollowly off the walls of the huge main room, where the head of a dinosaur skeleton nearly reached the second-floor ceiling. Ranged around the sides of the room were brightly colored carousel horses, looking oddly lifeless separated from their merry-go-rounds.

Nikki scanned the many hallways leading to other parts of the building and wondered if she should go back to the desk and get a map. Then, through the doorway of one of the side rooms, she caught sight of the Indian tepee and knew she was close.

She turned a corner and there it was—the display she was looking for. White drawings of babies from conception to birth. She gazed at the wall for a minute, then turned away, disappointed.

There's nothing here I haven't already seen in the brochures.

Then she stopped. Off to the right was another part of the display, and Nikki stepped back involuntarily when she saw it. There, in glass cubes set into the wall, were life-size forms of the brochure pictures. Each lighted cube was filled with liquid. And submerged in each cube was the body of a tiny baby. Nikki felt the blood rush to her face as she swallowed hard and forced herself to move closer.

The first two cubes contained babies from the earliest weeks of development. Nikki gazed at them, but the figures were so small that she had trouble seeing them. She went on to the third cube, the one labeled "Two Months."

Here there was a uterus cut down the middle and laid open as though hinged at the bottom. A child lay cradled in the top half, a perfect miniature of the babies at the hospital. The walls of the uterus looked thick, secure. Nikki thought how dark and warm it would be inside, the best of places for a delicate, grow-ing creature to hide.

In the fourth cube, labeled "Two and a Half Months," the baby was perhaps two inches long, still so fragile that the faintest breath would wound it. The small white body hung in the solu-tion upright, its back toward Nikki.

Every detail of that back was perfect. The midsection, the chest and belly, were rounded and full, narrowing to little hips. Nikki leaned even closer to see. From those hips dangled thread-like legs, yet legs unmistakably, with knees and feet. One small arm extended to the side, and through the translucent skin, she could see the two large bones of the forearm, bleached whiter than the tissue surrounding them.

And the hand—Nikki sucked in her breath—each of the five first knuckles were mere dots that seemed to glow through the skin. The fingers were minute, perfectly formed, each the size of a capital I without its crossbars. As she studied the child, Nikki could distinguish the faint outline of every rib inside that rounded abdomen.

Nikki jammed her hands into the pockets of her shorts to still their trembling. Her right eyelid started to twitch, and she walked quickly away from the cubes, stumbling into the Indian display. It was all true then—what she'd seen in the brochures. Only worse. These ... *things* ... weren't pictures; they were real.

She stopped in front of the tepee and stared, unseeing, at the Indian figures grouped around an electric campfire.

She had to see the display one more time. *You're crazy, Nikki,* she told herself. *Don't even go near those things again*. But before she could stop herself, she was standing in front of the glass cubes once more.

That's what it looks like, right now, inside me. Before, when she had tried to picture it, she'd imagined only a blunt-featured kind of blob, a sort of space creature with no real human features. But this . . . this was like the little plastic dolls she used to have for her doll house—every feature, every detail right where it belonged.

Nikki turned and rushed out the front doors of the museum.

Back at the hospital, no one wanted to talk. Grandpa sat stroking Gram's hand. Mrs. Sheridan gazed out the window at the hills beyond the city, sipping from a steaming paper cup of coffee. No one asked Nikki where she'd been.

When it was time to leave, Nikki could tell from her mother's stiff good-bye to Grandpa that she had come out on the losing end of the argument. At first she felt only relief that the flu question seemed to have been forgotten in the process. But when they stopped at the last red light before the expressway and Nikki's mother turned to look at her, she remembered the lesson she'd learned through years of observing her parents. It never took Rachel Sheridan long to find a new target for her anger and frustration. She was always most dangerous when she lost.

Nikki waited, on guard, all the way home from the hospital, but her mother said only, "Nicole, will you please stop making that clicking noise?"

Nikki looked down and found she'd been snapping the catch of her watch open and shut, over and over. She folded her hands tightly in her lap. The trick was to make herself as invisible as possible.

By the next morning, Nikki decided she must have misjudged. Perhaps, this one time, her mother would find some other way to deal with her anger, instead of venting it on Nikki.

But Nikki kept looking over her shoulder just in case. And when her mother finally struck, it was at the worst possible moment.

❧ *Eleven* ❧

NIKKI HAD JUST FINISHED her daily round of morning sickness. She wiped a cool washcloth across her damp face and gave the toilet one more cautionary flush to cover the last few dry heaves. When she turned around to leave the room, her mother stood in the doorway, watching.

Nikki opened her mouth, but she couldn't think of a single word to say.

"Another bout with the flu, dear?" Rachel moved to block the bathroom doorway, crossing her arms in front of her.

"What are you doing, spying on me like this?" Nikki burst out.

Her mother's mouth tightened. "Maybe you'd better come downstairs, and we'll talk about what I'm doing. Or more to the point, what *you're* doing." She pulled the bathroom door closed in Nikki's face and left.

Nikki stood absolutely still.

She knows. She knows!

Nikki started to shake violently, and then there were more

dry heaves, great spasms swelling up from her stomach that left her leaning, limp, against the sink.

When it ended, and she'd taken as long as she could to clean up, there was nothing to do but go downstairs. She tried to maneuver by being the first to attack.

Walking into the kitchen, she said, "So, whatever happened to the idea that bathrooms are private, that it's rude to open the door on someone?" Nikki opened the refrigerator and grabbed a carton of orange juice.

"I thought I'd better check on you, dear, especially when I heard you throwing up for the third morning in a row." Mrs. Sheridan wrapped the string around her steaming tea bag, squeezed the last brown drops from it, and laid the spent bag on her saucer. "Sit down, Nicole. I think it's time we talked."

Nikki sank onto a wooden chair, her shoulders slumped forward over the table.

"You're pregnant, aren't you?"

"Oh, come off it. A person gets sick for a few days, and the first thing you do is jump to conclusions. . . ."

"Don't play games with me, Nicole."

"Mother . . ."

"Stop acting like I'm some idiot on the street! You look like death warmed over, you've lost weight, you're throwing up every morning. And very obviously trying to hide it with all that flushing, by the way. How far along are you?"

Nikki felt like a caged animal. She could almost hear the door slam shut. "Almost nine weeks," she answered finally, her eyes fixed on her juice glass.

"And which of your charming friends has the distinction of being the father? Or don't you know?"

"Stop it! I don't have to take this from you or anyone else."

"Oh, really? I'll find out, you know, whether you tell me or not."

"You don't have to find out anything. It was T.J., okay? T.J.! And he's the only one it could be. He's the only guy I've ever slept with. And we only did it once!"

Her mother raised her eyebrows. "How original."

Nikki sprang out of the chair, her breath coming hard and fast.

"In fact," Mrs. Sheridan continued, "I think I've heard that line somewhere before."

Nikki was never sure, afterward, whether she dropped the glass or threw it. Either way, feeling it crash to splinters against the floor did only a little to satisfy the rage inside her.

"I really thought we'd taught you better than this, Nicole."

"Don't you get all moralistic with me!" Nikki shouted. "When did you ever say anything to me about sex? In fact, when did you ever have time to talk to me at all?"

"Lower your voice, Nicole. I have no intention of being shouted at. The question's not one of morals so much as brains. What good are all those sex education courses at the high school if you don't even know enough to use birth control?"

Nikki missed a beat, staring at her mother. "You're upset that I got caught. You don't care whether I slept with him or not. You're just mad that I got caught!"

"I think you'd better sweep up that glass."

There was silence between them until Nikki reached under the sink to grab the dustpan and whisk broom. When she had tipped the dustpan full of glass fragments into the wastebasket, her mother asked, "What do you plan to do about it?"

Nikki stood for a moment, staring out the kitchen window to the shore where the waves rolled in and the gulls cried. To tell her plans was to give her mother control. "I don't know. I haven't decided."

"At nine weeks, you don't have very long to make up your mind. I understand 12 weeks is pretty much the cut-off point."

"So, maybe . . . maybe I don't want to get an abortion."

"Oh, stop being such a child. What are you going to do, raise the baby yourself? Let's get one thing straight right now. I'm not the granny type. I have no intention of putting my next 15 years into raising your child."

"I didn't ask you to raise my child. I wouldn't let you any-where near my child!" Nikki's voice broke and she stopped, amazed at how quickly her mother could reduce her to a five-year-old again. She took a deep breath. *Get hold of yourself, Nikki. You're 16. Stop letting her yank you around this way.*

It took all her effort, but when she spoke again, her voice held steady. "I'm considering all the options, and when I decide, I'll let you know." She turned to go, but stopped short at the sound of her mother's laugh.

"Options? You really think a girl in this situation has any options?" Mrs. Sheridan leaned her forehead against the heel of her hand, shaking her head in disbelief. "I know you think I'm being harsh with you, Nicole, but I'm just telling you the facts. You can have this baby and see the next 20 years of your life go down the drain, or you can take care of the problem right now. Those are your options. I only wish someone had told *me*."

Rachel raised her head, and Nikki saw there were tears in her mother's eyes. She stared for a moment, then pushed open the screen door and fled.

Though it was only midmorning, the heat on the dune was already intense. The forest surrounded her with a green stillness as she climbed the boardwalk steps, and it was a balm to all the hurting places inside her.

Nikki stopped frequently along the trail, taking deep breaths of the woody air and listening to the liquid song of a robin that echoed now and then under the canopy of leaves.

She leaned over the weathered board railing, staring down at the plants without really seeing them. Instead, she saw herself walking here as a child with Grandpa, his steady hands pointing out different trees and plants, his whistle imitating the bird songs. He'd made her laugh when he pointed out the polypode ferns because she thought the name was funny.

"Polypode," he had said again, for the pleasure of hearing her giggle. "Polyploidy." She'd giggled harder, trying to say the words after him. "Polypetalous..." Their laughter pealed through the forest together, and when she had caught her breath, she urged him on.

"More, Grandpa, do more!"

He frowned down at her, trying to look stern. "What do I look like? A walking dictionary?" But the corner of his mouth twitched, and she had made him say the words over and over for her, in a kind of singsong.

But there was no laughter this summer, with Grandpa trying for a miracle at Gram's bedside, and Nikki carrying her secret alone. Well, not exactly alone anymore, though that would have been easier. She had wanted to tell someone, sharing the burden, but her mother's knowing only added more weight to her shoulders.

Nikki ducked under the railing and stepped across the dry sandy soil to the foot of the great oak. She sat just the way she had the week before, the day she'd found out for sure she was pregnant, with her back against the broad tree trunk, staring out at the lake.

Now that her mother knew, things would only get worse. She would push Nikki to get an abortion. *Well, that's what I want, too, isn't it? At least, I thought I did.*

It was supposed to be so simple. Just have the abortion and get on with life. People did it all the time. But it wasn't turning out that way at all.

"I wouldn't let you near my child!" she had screamed at Mother in the kitchen. In some way, since those horrible few minutes in the museum, the thing growing inside her had taken on the form of a child, like the tiny white bodies in the display case. She could see it in her mind.

Nikki pulled her knees up to her chest and rested her forehead against them. *I should have just made them do the abortion the day I found out. I should never have waited. Then it would all be over, fixed, settled.* Now she had to think about it, make some kind of choice. And no matter which way she chose, somebody was going to get hurt.

"Nikki?"

She jerked her head up. Jeff Allen stood on the sand beside her in his usual cut-offs and T-shirt, sunlight playing across his face and dark hair as the leaves shifted above him.

"Nik, do you mind if I sit down?"

"Sure. I mean no, go ahead." All she could think was, *My face must be a disaster from all that crying.* She wiped quickly at her eyes, pushed the hair back behind her ears.

Jeff settled himself on the ground beside her, and Nikki looked at his long legs, at the dark hairs springing from his tanned calves, the muscles firm from years of playing basketball. She felt him watching her, and she looked away quickly.

They sat without speaking, staring ahead at the hazy blue lake dotted with morning sailboats. The brightly colored sails tacked back and forth like butterflies in the wind, barely skimming the surface of the water.

"Nikki, why don't you just tell me what's bothering you?"

"I don't know what you're talking about."

"Come off it. We've been friends since we learned to talk. I think by now I know you well enough to tell when something's wrong. This past week, you've been off in some world of your own."

"My grandmother had a stroke, remember? Or doesn't that count?"

Jeff picked up a stick from the ground beside him and began methodically stripping the leaves and twigs from its sides.

"Yeah, it counts. But you're snowing me. There was something wrong way before she had the stroke. That first morning at breakfast, and when we were down at Rosie's for a Coke, and on the Fourth ... Nikki, do you think I'm so dumb I can't put two and two together?"

She stared at him, silent, then looked away again.

"Well?"

"Look, I'm sorry, Jeff. I shouldn't have made that crack about Gram's stroke. But I don't know what you're talking about. You know I had the flu. . . ."

"Aw, stop it, Nik!" Jeff flung the stick to the ground in front of him. "If we can't talk anymore, then fine, we won't talk. But don't give me any more of this junk about the 'flu.' Whatever's bothering you, it's a lot more than some lousy virus."

Nikki picked a blade of dried grass carefully off the hem of her shorts before she spoke. "I can't ... I don't ... know how to talk to you anymore. You're different this year. . . ." Tears welled up in her eyes, and she stopped, afraid they would spill over.

A green oak leaf drifted slowly down between them, spinning

lazily to the sand. In the silence, Nikki heard Jeff moving beside her, reaching into his pocket.

"Nikki, look at me."

She shook her head, swallowing hard.

"Nikki, this is Jeff, remember? The guy who helped you build sand castles, who taught you to ride a skateboard. . . ."

She shook her head again, blinking hard.

"The guy who always beats you when we swim to the pier. . . ."

"You don't!" she said, turning to look at him.

It was the old Jeff she saw sitting there, dark-rimmed glasses sliding down the bridge of his nose. He hitched them into place with the old familiar gesture.

"What . . . what are you . . . ?"

"I thought it might help you unload if I looked more, you know, like I used to," he answered quietly, "so I brought the glasses along. I'm not nuts about wearing them either, so would you please start talking to me again so I can take the stupid things off?" He grinned at her crookedly, his eyebrows raised over the dark frames, waiting for an answer.

Her laughter couldn't keep the tears from spilling over, and Jeff, still grinning, offered her the tail of his T-shirt with a flourish. "It's the best offer you're gonna get, out here in the wilds."

She pushed his hand away, still laughing. "You idiot, I'm not wiping my face on your shirt!" She brushed at the tears with both hands, drying her fingers on the denim fabric of her shorts and feeling better than she had all week.

"So," Jeff asked, "to use a famous line, can we talk?" He took off his glasses and put them in his pocket, then he picked up the stick again, his arms relaxed across his knees, and waited.

Nikki toyed with a loose string that dangled from her sock and tried to think how to say it, words to make it hurt less, but once she began, there was no choosing. They all spilled out in a rush.

"I was dating this guy, T.J., who I'd liked for a couple years. I don't know why, but he finally asked me out. And I acted so stupid—all starry-eyed and, oh, I don't know, I just thought he really cared about me. I guess I kind of made him into something he wasn't, in my mind, you know? He plays soccer and he's, oh, part of that crowd that runs things around school and, anyway, we were at this party after the Junior-Senior Banquet and he got drunk and—" from the corner of her eye, Nikki saw Jeff's hands go still "—uh, I, uh, let him, I mean, we had sex and . . ."

There was a sharp crack as the stick in Jeff's hand snapped in two.

For a second, there was silence, then Jeff reached to cover her hand with his. "You're gonna shred that sock if you don't quit."

Nikki looked down at her leg. The top of the sock hung loose and ragged, the elastic thread wound over and over around her finger. She snapped it loose and rolled the white rounds off her finger, then tossed them in the leaves.

When he spoke again, Jeff's voice was quiet. "So now you're pregnant?"

Nikki nodded.

"Do you know what you're going to do?"

She turned to him then, her blue eyes brimming. She tried to speak, but no sound came. She spread her hands, palms up, and shook her head.

When he put out his arms, all the walls came down inside her. She leaned against his chest and sobbed, and he held her gently, asking nothing, rubbing her back, and stroking her dark hair as her body shook against his shoulder.

"It's okay, Nik, it's okay," he murmured over and over, a

little litany of comfort. "It's all right, it's okay." It went on for a long time. She hadn't known just how much she needed to cry with someone.

Eventually, when her sobs had faded to small hiccuping sniffles, he spoke. "Guys can be such jerks."

"I wasn't exactly brilliant myself, letting this happen." She straightened up a little, wiping at her eyes again. "Seems like all I do is cry these days ... when I'm not throwing up everything down to my toenail polish," she added.

"Nikki, does anyone else know?"

"My mother just found out this morning. She heard me throwing up the last couple mornings and figured out what's going on. We had a rotten fight. I think she just wants me to have an abortion and pretend the whole thing never happened."

"So are you going to?"

She thought for a minute, growing more and more uneasy at the sweet scent of his aftershave. She moved away a little before she spoke. "When I found out for sure last week, on the way up here, I was so panicked that I decided an abortion was the only way out. But now I'm not so sure, Jeff."

"Why not?"

"When I went to do it—have the abortion, I mean—there were all these crazy demonstrators in front of the clinic, yelling stuff at me."

"What kind of stuff?"

"Oh, about it being a child and not to kill it. And they gave me some pamphlets ..."

"The ones you had in the car?" he asked.

"Yeah."

"That's why you were so upset at Rosie's, wasn't it?"

She nodded. "I'm sorry I lied to you, Jeff. I feel like I've done more lying this past week than in the rest of my life put together. But how can I tell people the truth? I mean, it's not exactly dinner conversation. 'Oh, by the way, I'm about two months pregnant. Just thought you'd like to know!'

"Anyway," she continued, "I was going to go right back the next day, to the abortion clinic, but then Gram had the stroke and it was the Fourth. And then my parents came and, well, you know what's been going on since then. Now I don't even get to use my car because my mother needs it, so I can't drive to the clinic. And I looked at those pamphlets the demonstrators gave me, and they made me wonder about this whole thing. And then what really got to me was yesterday. Do you remember a long time ago, when Grandpa took you and Carly and me to the museum in town?"

Jeff nodded, watching her.

"Well, do you remember the display about how babies develop, before they're born?"

"The one with the babies in those little glass boxes? I don't remember it from that time we went with your grandpa, but my parents took us to the museum last year, and I saw it then."

"Jeff, when I looked at those, I could see every little rib, even the knuckles in the hands. And that's what I figure this baby, the one inside me, looks like right now. So how can I . . . just . . . kill something like that?"

Jeff ran his hand over his chin, frowning. He looked out toward the lake, his eyes following the line of a jet ski weaving noisily between the silent sailboats, the water rising in a foaming wake behind it.

"I don't know, Nik. I don't know." He paused for moment before continuing. "We talk about it a lot at home—abortion, I mean."

"Well?"

"Well, Dad always talks about life being a continuum. And if that's so, then I don't see where you can break in and say for sure, 'This thing isn't a person yet, so today it's okay to kill it.'" He shifted his weight a little, eased a pine cone out from under him, and tossed it into the thick, green ferns.

"Yeah, but how can you say something that tiny, that unfinished, really is a person?" she said. "I mean, it can't take care of itself, it can't even live without someone else doing every single thing for it."

"What about your grandmother, Nik? She can't take care of herself right now. Isn't she still a person?"

Nikki chewed at her bottom lip, her eyes narrowing.

"And besides," Jeff went on, "what does size have to do with it anyway? Maybe, because they're so tiny, these fetuses—babies, whatever you want to call them—ought to be more protected, because they can't fend for themselves yet, you know?"

"Jeff, you sound just like one of those demonstrators! You really think it'd be wrong to get an abortion, don't you?"

"I'm not telling you what to do, Nikki. I'm just telling you what I think. Besides, you said yourself you weren't sure anymore. Maybe you should take your time, think about it some more."

"Oh, right, and in the meantime, get big as a house and keep throwing up every morning and have the whole world find out how stupid I was? That kind of time, you mean?"

"Hey, don't get mad at me, Nik. I'm just trying to think it through with you. What about this other life? Doesn't this kid even get a chance? I mean, I think when God starts a life, we have to respect that."

Nikki got to her feet abruptly and brushed the dirt off the seat of her shorts. "Don't bring God into this," she said frowning. She stuffed both hands into her pockets and looked back down at Jeff.

"You know what? All of a sudden, I feel like there's way too many people involved in this decision. I mean, until this morning, it was entirely up to me. Now my mother's trying to get in on it, and you. And now God, too." She shook her head slowly, bewildered.

Jeff unfolded his long legs to stand beside her. She could see his glasses stretching the pocket of his shorts out of shape. She thought about all he'd done, and she smiled up at him.

"Thanks, though, for trying to help. I wanted to talk to you all week. I just couldn't make myself do it."

"Looks to me like I did more harm than good."

"Just give me some time, okay? At least you listened. That's what I really needed."

Jeff's face relaxed into a slow, warm smile. "Hey, that's me. Free listening, free advice, whatever."

As they made their way toward the boardwalk, Nikki asked, "Did I ever tell you I used to be jealous of Carly, when we were kids?" She ducked under the railing and climbed back up onto the wooden walkway.

"Jealous? Why?"

"You guys always had each other to talk to. I used to wish you were my big brother."

Nikki turned and started down the steps, but Jeff hung back, silent for a moment, his dark eyes intent on her back. Then he kicked the wooden corner post hard, winced, and started down the walk behind her.

When they reached the house, the garage stood empty, the garage door wide open.

"My mother must have gone in to the hospital," Nikki said. "Looks like I got left behind."

"I can drive you in if you want," Jeff said, holding the door of the screened porch open for her. Nikki tried to step over Gallie, who lay in a bright pool of sunlight on the middle of the porch floor, but she tripped and grabbed the chain of the porch swing to steady herself.

"Gallie, you're right in the way," Nikki said, laughing as she nudged at the dog with her sandaled foot. "Go on, move over a little."

Jeff dropped into one of the white wicker rockers and wiped sweat off his forehead with the back of his hand. "Whew, it's going to be another scorcher."

"Jeff."

He opened his eyes and looked up at the sound of her voice. "What's the matter? You sick again?"

Nikki shook her head, and her eyes narrowed as she reached down to rub Gallie's ears. "This is the first time Gallie's come out of Gram's room since the stroke. I mean, besides when we use the leash and make him go outside. He's been lying right in their bedroom doorway since the ambulance took Gram away."

"Yeah, I know." Jeff got out of the chair and knelt down on one knee beside the dog. "We had an awful time getting him to go outside when you were in Grand Rapids."

"Jeff, I know this sounds crazy, but do you think it could mean something's changed? With Gram?"

Jeff rolled his eyes. "No, I think it means Gallie's sick and tired of lying in the bedroom and decided to get some sun. Right, fella?" He stroked the burnished fur, and the dog looked up at him with moist, brown eyes, the feathery tip of his tail thumping the floor softly.

"Jeff, be serious. You don't think Gram could've . . . " Nikki broke off.

"Died?" Jeff asked softly. "Come on, Nik, you're getting all upset over nothing. This isn't the Twilight Zone. Old Gallie just wanted a change of scene."

Jeff sank back into the rocker and stretched his legs out in front of him, but Nikki stood still in the middle of the porch, staring at the golden retriever. Gallie, glad to be the center of attention, laid his shaggy head companionably across Nikki's sandal and thumped his tail even harder.

"Okay, so it's crazy, all right? But I can't help it. I think something happened at the hospital. I have to call and find out."

Nikki started for the kitchen, and as she did, the phone rang loudly inside. She jerked the door open and grabbed the receiver off the counter. Jeff was right behind her.

"Hello?" Grandpa's voice came over the line. "Rachel? Nikki?"

"It's Nikki. Mother already left. What's going on, Grandpa? Is Gram all right?"

"She's more than all right. She's awake, Nikki. About a half hour ago. She's out of the coma!"

Nikki could hardly take in the words at first, but the meaning of them unfolded inside her with a glowing warmth. She felt a smile spread over her face as he talked.

"Grandpa, hang on," she said and turned to Jeff, who was sitting on the kitchen counter beside her.

"Gram woke up! She came out of the coma." She nodded toward Gallie, who sat on the kitchen floor between them, his tail fanning the tile floor wildly. "I *told* you it meant something happened!"

"I could swear he's grinning," Jeff said, watching the dog and shaking his head back and forth.

Nikki spoke into the phone. "I'm coming right in, Grandpa. Jeff said he'd drive me."

She listened silently as Grandpa relayed more news and her smile faded as she took in his words. "I understand, Grandpa. See you in a bit."

"What's wrong?" Jeff asked, as she laid the phone back on the counter. "You got awfully serious all of a sudden."

"He just said to remember this doesn't mean Gram's back to normal. She's awake and all, but she still can't talk. And she's paralyzed some. They can't tell how much yet."

Jeff slid off the counter and stood in front of Nikki. "But she's awake. That's what counts right now. The rest, the talking and stuff, that can all come back later, with therapy."

Nikki swallowed hard and nodded. "You're right, Jeff. I'll just be glad for what we've got." She took a tissue from the box on the counter and blew her nose. "Are you sure you can drive me in?"

"Absolutely. Let me go tell Mom and Dad. They need to hear the good news anyway."

Jeff steered the Bronco into the semicircular driveway at the hospital and shifted into park in front of the sliding glass doors. He shook his head at Nikki's invitation to come in with her.

"This is a family time, Nikki. I don't want to butt in. Besides, we're all coming in this evening to visit."

Nikki slid down from the seat, then turned back to face him. "Thanks, Jeff. For everything."

"Hey, like I said before, whenever you need me." He grinned

and shifted into drive, and Nikki watched him ease the vehicle back into traffic.

When she hurried through the door of her grandmother's room, her first thought was that Grandpa had made a mistake. Everything looked exactly the same. Gram lay perfectly still, her eyes closed. But no mistake could have set off the look of pure joy she saw in Grandpa's eyes when he rose to hug her. Even Nikki's mother was smiling from her seat at the foot of the bed, the morning's argument apparently forgotten. Gram opened her eyes at the sound of their conversation, and Nikki went to her side.

"Gram? Gram, it's me, Nikki."

Gram's blue eyes wandered in her direction for a few seconds, then suddenly slid into focus.

"She's very weak, Nikki. It takes her longer than usual to respond," Grandpa said from just behind Nikki's shoulder.

Nikki bent over the bed, bracing herself carefully against the metal bedrail, and kissed her grandmother on the forehead. The blue eyes looked at her intently.

"Gram, I'm so glad you're back! I knew something was going on when Gallie left your bedroom and came downstairs. I knew you must be getting better." She didn't mention the other possibility she'd considered.

At the mention of Gallie, the muscles of Gram's face began to work. At first, Nikki thought she was in pain. The right side of her mouth turned up. The left side sagged limply, and the skin under her left eye hung loose and puffy. Nikki saw then that Gram was trying to smile.

She'd never realized before how much a smile depended on a person's eyes. But even in this funny, lopsided grimace, the light showed through in Gram's blue eyes. She was trapped in silence, but she was still there.

Nikki didn't know whether to laugh or cry, so she leaned over and hugged her grandmother gently, careful not to jostle the bed.

❧ *Twelve* ❧

THE HUMID HEAT OF THE NIGHT before had congealed into a thick, gray fog. It sculpted the beach into a foreign landscape, blotting out sight of the long, stone pier and even the bright, pulsing flash of the lighthouse. Only the low rhythmic throb of the foghorn carried through it.

Nikki couldn't see 10 feet in front of her, but she kept going, cautiously, her eyes fixed on the bit of beach just ahead of her feet. *Funny*, she thought, trying to keep her breathing even, *how as soon as one situation begins to resolve itself, the other one comes back in full force.*

She had checked again, in front of the mirror this morning. The slight bulge was unmistakable now, right over the elastic of her bikini panties. This time, it wasn't the wavy glass of the mirror that distorted her image. No matter how she turned, her stomach definitely pudged out.

Oh, great, she'd thought as she stood looking at her reflection. *I lose five pounds, and my stomach gets bigger. Exercise—that had to help, for a while at least.*

Back in Ohio, jogging had always been an easy way to stay in shape. And when things got bad at home, a half hour run through the park seemed to wipe away the tension. Nikki tried to settle into the easy pace she was used to but found she could no longer keep it up. The nausea stole her breath away, and every few minutes, she had to slow to a walk, gulping in great draughts of damp air before she could go on.

Waves licked at the shoreline, hissing softly over the rocky sand, but they were only sounds in the ghostly fog as Nikki's feet pounded past. The thin cries of gulls pierced the air from the sky overhead, but they flew unseen. It was eerie, unreal, the whole situation out of sync with the fury that erupted and swelled inside her as she ran, driving her feet faster, faster.

One mistake. One time, and my whole life goes down the drain. She pressed her hand hard against the cramp in her side. *I can't even jog anymore. I can't get through one lousy morning without puking all over the place. And now it's starting to show. How long do I have till everyone knows?*

It's not fair! Her feet beat out the rhythm as she ran—not fair, not fair, not fair. *What about the kids at school who sleep around all the time? What about T.J.? Everything's ruined for me—everything!—and he gets off scot-free.*

Forget the pictures. Forget the museum. She had to get to the clinic. It was the only way out, the only way back to normal.

Nikki glanced down. The lace on her right shoe slapped wetly against the sand, and she stooped to tie it, breathing fast as she knelt. Her hands shook a little, but even so, her fingers knotted and pulled precisely. And in that moment, her mind conjured up the image of the tiny, white hand of the baby in the museum display, the whole hand no bigger than her thumbnail, the hand that would never tie a shoe.

Stop it, stop it, stop it! Nikki sprang to her feet and sprinted hard across the beach. The loose, dry sand slowed her down, and she veered back toward the water, where the sand was wet and packed. She counted steps, counted breaths, anything to shut out the thoughts that hounded her.

Finally, when she couldn't manage another step, another breath, she slowed again. She felt the soggy rubbing inside her shoes where waves had washed over her feet and soaked her socks.

I can do what I want! she shouted silently at the sand, at the waves, at the fog, at everything around her. *I can do what I want, and you can't stop me!* "I think when God starts a life, we need to respect that," Jeff had said. Well, she hadn't been sure about God for a long time now—whether He was there or not. So as far as she could see, this was her decision and hers alone.

"I'll tell you what choices a girl has," her mother's voice echoed in her head. "You can have this baby and see the next 20 years of your life go down the drain. . . ."

No! she thought. *I have to think about me. My whole life's ahead of me, the rest of high school, college, getting married. I want those things, too, just like everyone else!*

The shape of a boat emerged dimly on the beach ahead, a sail-boat from one of the dune houses. Its sails were down, rolled neatly, and the little craft sat lifeless where beach grass invaded the sand.

Nikki stumbled to it and dropped onto the bow. Leaning forward, with her knees spread wide apart and her hands braced against them, she sucked in deep breaths. Gradually, her heart slowed its pounding, and her breathing calmed.

You've got to help. You have to help me decide what to do.

Who are you talking to? You don't even believe in God, right? So who are you talking to?

I must be losing my mind.

Help me. Please, please help me!

With a start, Nikki felt the warm, golden fur of Gallie's head thrust between her knees, his wet tongue lapping her cheek and hands in a frenzy of affection. From the white mist behind the dog, Grandpa materialized. He had on his old knit sweater and brown pants, the clothes he always wore to walk Gallie on the beach in chilly weather. A few strands of gray hair lifted across his forehead in the damp breeze. He smiled at Nikki's surprise.

"Sorry, honey, I didn't mean to startle you." He lowered himself onto the bow beside her with a small grunt. "It's good to be out on the beach again. This is the first walk I've taken since Carole's stroke."

Nikki nodded. They sat together for a few minutes, saying nothing, watching as Gallie raced back and forth from the sailboat to the water's edge, until the fur on his legs dripped dark with water. He stopped only long enough to bark madly at a gull that dropped from the fog overhead and then went mincing flatfooted down the beach, probing the sand for edible scraps.

Nikki heard the foghorn sound over and over, a deep contralto vibration in the air that reminded her of her own worrisome thoughts.

Shifting his weight cautiously on the fiberglass craft, Grandpa nodded toward the dog. "He's overjoyed to be out of the house. This has been a tough time for him. I can't figure how animals know when something's terribly wrong, but they do. Some extra sense we don't even understand, I guess."

He waited, but Nikki said nothing.

"It's been a hard week for you, too, Nikki."

"Well, sure. Gram's stroke has been hard on everyone."

"No, that's not what I mean." He reached across the bow and covered her hand with his own bent fingers. "Nikki, honey—" he squeezed gently "—I know."

She turned to meet his eyes.

"Mother told you?" she cried, her voice tight, distorted from the effort of holding back the tears.

"No, no." He held up his other hand, his fingers splayed slightly, to ward off her anger. "Your mother didn't say a word."

"Then how ...?"

"Your grandmother told me."

Nikki narrowed her eyes, staring at him intently. "Wait a minute. Gram doesn't even know. And she can't talk, anyway."

"She does know, honey. I'm not sure how, but she does. And she's very concerned about you."

Nikki's thoughts flew back to that first day at the hospital, when she couldn't hold the pain inside any longer and had spilled out her story. So Gram *had* heard. Somehow, it had gotten through to her.

When Nikki didn't respond, he continued. "You're right, of course. She can't talk ... but she can write a little. The writing's not real clear, but I got the point." He took off his steel-rimmed glasses and wiped droplets of moisture from the lenses onto his shirt. He settled the glasses once more on the bridge of his nose.

"Anyway, how I know is not the important issue here. You're what's important. I'd like you to tell me about it. Would you do that, Nikki?"

The gentle pressure of his hand released the words dammed up inside, and he kept his hand on hers while she spoke, encouraging her when her voice broke. At last the whole story was out, and there was silence for a moment.

"Have you told anyone else? Or have you been carrying

this all alone while the rest of us were all wrapped up with your grandmother?"

"I told Jeff yesterday." She sniffled a little.

"Jeff's a good man."

"Yeah. He's grown up a lot this year. He said some things that really made me think."

"Such as?"

"Oh, we talked about . . . well, about what I should do." She couldn't bring herself to say the word to him.

"You're thinking about an abortion?" he asked.

Nikki shrugged helplessly. "It's the only thing that makes any sense for me, Grandpa. I mean, what am I supposed to do? Give up the rest of my life because of one mistake? It's not fair!" She turned to look at him.

His dark eyebrows shadowed his eyes as he watched her intently.

"You think abortion's wrong, don't you?" she asked.

"I think," he spoke slowly, choosing his words with great care, "that you don't correct one mistake by making another."

"See?" She slid off the boat and began to pace back and forth on the sand, her arms crossed tight over her chest. "You *do* think it's wrong! Well, *I* think it's wrong for me to have to lose out on the next 20 years of my life just because of one mistake."

"Whoa, whoa, Nikki." He held up his hands, motioning for her to calm down. "Why all the anger? You asked for my opinion, remember?"

She took a deep breath. "I'm sorry, Grandpa. But it's like you don't even realize abortion is okay now. Things are different from when you were young."

"And I think you know very well that I'm aware of the legal status of abortion." He paused for a moment, then patted the boat's fiberglass bow beside him. "Why don't you come sit back down?"

Nikki stood staring at him for a moment, then gave in and sat next to him.

"You're carrying a lot of anger, honey," he said.

"I know. I'm not even sure why I'm yelling at you. It's not your fault."

"When a person's full of anger, it splashes out a little onto anyone who comes close. I know. I was angry a lot of the time in the hospital this past week."

Nikki stared at him. "You?" She gave a short laugh. "You didn't act like it."

"I think the key is finding out who you're really angry at and going to them directly."

"Well, that's easy. T.J. was such a jerk!" she said, shaking her head. "But there's no way I'm talking to him. He'd think it was a big joke, and it'd be all over town in a couple days."

"I didn't mean that you should talk to T.J."

"But you just said . . . What *are* you saying, anyway?"

"That I don't think your real anger's directed at a person. I think you're angry at God."

"Angry at God!" She threw the words back at him. "I'm not even sure I believe in God anymore." She picked up a piece of driftwood that lay beside the hull and jabbed it into the sand between her feet, making little holes that filled in with wet sand as fast as she made them. "How can you be so sure He's even there, Grandpa? I mean, how can you just totally disagree with all the people who say there's no God?"

"I guess because what they believe doesn't match what I see all around me—the mystery, the beauty, the magic," he said. "I'm a biologist, honey. I can't ignore the proofs I see every day that someone was behind all of this. And unless I'm way off base, in the final analysis, it's Him you're angry with, Nikki. Don't you hear it in your words—'It's not fair'? I think we all expect someone to govern the way things happen in this world, to be in charge. If no one seems to be doing that, we feel this sense of injustice, the kind I suspect you're feeling."

Nikki drew a grid in the sand and filled in the squares with X's and O's. Gallie came running and slid to a stop just in front of her, sending sand flying in all directions. The dog's heavy warmth pressed against her legs, and Nikki stroked him absently until her hand touched the dripping fur on his sides.

"Yuk! Go on, Gallie, you're getting me all wet." She pushed with both hands, and Gallie bounded off again. "So how do you just tell God you're angry at Him? I mean, isn't it wrong to do that? Assuming I did start believing in Him, that is." She brushed the wet sand off her thighs and hands.

"You might try reading Job, or Jeremiah, or some of the psalms King David wrote. They all seemed to think it was okay to express their feelings honestly. Nikki, God gave us the capacity to have feelings. Do you really think it shocks Him when we do?"

The foghorn bellowed in the distance, its hollow throb muffled by the layer of heavy fog.

Nikki straightened up. "Fine. Okay. So what if God really is there? That still doesn't solve my problem, does it? I just get it all figured out in my mind—what I'm going to do about being pregnant—then people confuse me."

"How's that?"

"Well, when I went back to the clinic in Howellsville, the demonstrators gave me some pamphlets that showed what the baby looks like inside me. After that, I started to wonder if it was right to do this. But there's a law—I mean, it's legal—so doesn't that mean it's okay?"

Grandpa watched her silently, waiting. Nikki went on.

"Then remember the day you and Mother were arguing at the hospital? I went back to the museum where you took Jeff and Carly and me a long time ago. And I looked at that display about the babies. You know, those ones in the little cubes?" Nikki's voice made a small choking sound, and Grandpa put his arm around her. "And now I don't know what to think." She bit at the skin of her bottom lip.

"Nikki, honey, I don't really think you're confused because of what other people are telling you. I think you've seen enough to know what's right. It's just that either way you go, there's pain involved."

"But what if I don't believe it's a child?" she asked. "Nobody ever talks about it being a child. It's just tissue or something."

Grandpa shook his head. "I can't look at a fetus as just a piece of tissue. It's far too complex, too much of a wonder for that. I see the image of a maker stamped all over it."

"Grandpa, I don't know what to think anymore. All I know is that, while I'm trying to make up my mind, I'm starting to show. I have to decide what to do, and fast. I can't go back to school pregnant. And I can't raise a child. I mean, I'm 16! How would I support it? I wouldn't know what to do if it got sick or . . ."

"You're right, Nikki. No one expects that. But I don't think you're looking at all the options. I know Jeff's dad works with some adoption agencies in Chicago. Have you ever thought about adoption?"

"No." She picked up the driftwood and began to smooth Gallie's paw prints from the sand in front of her. When she had rubbed them flat, she answered quietly. "I couldn't do that anyway. Go through the whole pregnancy and all and then just . . . hand the baby over to someone else. You never even get to know who adopts it, do you?"

"That's not really true anymore. If you have an open adoption, I think you can choose the family and get pictures every so often."

"Still, how could I just give it away?" She looked directly at him, and the pain stood naked in her eyes. "There's no way I can keep a baby, but I'm getting to the point where I don't think I can live with myself if I have an abortion. And now I have to think about going through the whole thing and then giving the baby away?" She got to her feet again and tossed the stick as far as she could toward the water, but it fell silently out of sight into the thick fog.

"Nikki, there's no easy way out of this. There's going to be pain no matter what you decide. But this baby bears no responsibility for what's happened. Should it have to die just because, simply by being there, it causes trouble for you?"

Nikki didn't answer.

"Some women carry the effects of an abortion all their lives. What looks like the simplest answer now may turn out to cause you the most trouble in the long run." He hesitated. "Then, too, I have a certain responsibility to my great-grandchild."

Gallie dashed to Grandpa's side, spraying water across his pants. Grandpa busied himself brushing the sand out of the dog's coat. Nikki hung her head and closed her eyes. She wished she were dead.

❧ Thirteen ❧

NIKKI WAS EATING LUNCH on the back porch with her mother and Grandpa before the fog began to clear. Mrs. Sheridan had been so distracted by Gram's coming out of the coma that she hadn't brought up the matter of Nikki's pregnancy again. Yet.

But Nikki could see by the way she was acting that it was on her mind. Every time her mother glanced in her direction, Nikki steeled herself for what she knew was coming.

At least the weather was turning out better than she'd expected. One minute, the air was gray, and the porch seemed stuffy and closed-in; the next, a sudden brightening showed down near the water, and there stood the red lighthouse at the end of the pier, highlighted by a shaft of sunshine. Then all across the beach, fog began to melt, leaving ragged shreds here and there that shrank within minutes to wisps of damp smoke.

The phone rang in the kitchen, and Nikki hurried to answer it.

"Nikki? It's Jeff," the voice came over the line. "I called to see if you want to go with us this afternoon. The twins are begging to go climb Mt. Baldy and swim at Oval Beach and stuff, so Carly and I are gonna take them in the boat, soon as the foghorn stops."

Yes! Nikki thought, anxious to be out of the house and away from her mother. "What about your parents? Aren't they going?"

"Nah, they can't. You know how they always do some big project on the house every summer? Well, this year it's painting the kitchen. They're right in the middle of it—looks like they might finish some time next month."

Nikki heard voices and laughter in the background, and Jeff yelling, "Hey, knock it off! That thing is wet!" Then he was back on the line. "Sorry, Nik, didn't mean to holler in your ear. It's nuts here, like usual. So, you want to go?"

She hesitated for a moment. *If I keep a T-shirt on over my suit, my stomach won't show.* "Yeah, I'll come, Jeff. I'll be right over." She turned and headed for the stairs.

Jeff grinned with pleasure as the boat, called *Another Line*, sliced through the water like a quicksilver plow, foaming blue-gray ridges rising on either side. The boat was a small, trim, blue-and-white craft christened by Carl Allen, who got a huge laugh out of having his secretary tell people he was on *Another Line* when they called his office.

"Jeff!" Carly shouted.

He glanced back over his shoulder, startled. "What're you yelling for?"

"Because I've called you three times, but you're so busy playing captain you haven't heard a word. Did you bring sunscreen?"

"No, I thought you brought all that stuff."

"Great." Carly shook her head. "I'm in for another skin cancer lecture from Dad tonight."

Adam was leaning over the side of the boat, his hand extended, trying to reach into the wake.

"Adam, sit down, would you?" Jeff ordered.

Behind Jeff's back, Abby put her hands on her hips and mimicked his words to her twin.

"Don't forget I have a rearview mirror up here, squirt," Jeff said. "How'd you like to get dunked in the harbor when I dock?"

Nikki watched Jeff guide the boat easily through the channel. She couldn't help wondering what he thought of her after their conversation on the dune. *Probably that I'm an idiot*, she told herself, turning her head to look out across the open water. Still, Jeff had a way of surprising her, the way he came right out and said what was on his mind—stuff about God and respecting life, subjects that other guys steered clear of.

Nikki glanced in his direction again and was surprised to find him watching her. Twin red spots burned high on his cheekbones. He looked away quickly, but Nikki felt the boat speed up a little underneath her.

When they reached the harbor, Jeff tied up alongside a battered fishing boat, then held out his hand to help Carly and Nikki onto the boardwalk. Abby and Adam scrambled out on their own, tipping the boat so that it barely missed taking on water.

The dune known as Mt. Baldy rose straight up from the harbor, jutting in between the town of Saugatuck on one side and Lake Michigan on the other. The trail over the top of the dune and through the forest was a favorite hiking path, so a boardwalk had been built here also, like the one in Rosendale. They climbed the steep stairs, with Adam and Abby counting each step at the top of their lungs. By the time they yelled "Seventy-five!" even the twins were glad to sit and rest on the benches provided.

"Do you think Gram will get totally better now?" Abby asked as she sank onto the worn wood of the bench. The twins had long ago adopted Nikki's grandparents as their own, even calling them Gram and Grandpa.

From where he was sprawled across two steps, Adam added, "Yeah, you wouldn't want her to be like a . . . a zombie or something."

He saw the look that crossed Carly's face and tried to backtrack.

"Hey, I didn't mean a real zombie. I just mean all paralyzed and stuff. . . ."

"I know what you mean," Nikki answered, trying to ease his embarrassment. "To be honest, Adam, I guess that's what we're all worried about. That she'll be 'paralyzed and stuff.'" Adam smiled his relief, and Nikki continued. "I know the nurses and therapists work with her every day so her arms and legs don't stiffen up, and now that she's out of the coma, they're going to see how much she can move around on her own. Grandpa told me they expect her to need a wheelchair for quite a while."

"A wheelchair!" Abby made a face at the thought. "That's awful."

"I want one of those peach pies Gram makes again," Adam said. "What happens if she can't cook anymore?"

Jeff saw Nikki's mouth tighten. "Enough questions, you guys," he said. "Come on, we'll race you to the beach."

The change from cool green forest to hot, white sand was abrupt. The boardwalk ended in the trees on the crest of the hill, and suddenly there was nothing ahead but blue sky and blue-gray water, seamed together in a neat, straight line at the horizon. Hikers were left to scramble down the steep hill in the loose, dry sand any way they could.

Adam and Abby threw themselves into the trek with glee, running with exaggerated strides. Over and over they fell, slipping, stumbling down the face of the dune, the smooth, creamy sand sliding with them. Jeff was close behind. His long legs carried him faster, but he sank deeper into the sand with each step so that he struggled more in its grasp.

Carly and Nikki waited for a minute on the top of the dune. Far below, the beach was packed with swimmers and sunbathers. The salty smell of hot dogs and the sounds of children playing in the surf were caught on the lake breeze and tossed up to them. Bathing suits and towels splashed the hot, beige sand with every bright color.

Nikki and Carly turned and looked at each other. Then, in silent agreement, they both sat down and started to slide.

"We need one of those plastic sleds, those round ones," Carly yelled.

Nikki laughed and nodded, grabbing at a clump of beach grass as she slid helplessly past.

When Adam and Abby reached the beach, they chased each other into the water immediately. Carly and Jeff peeled off their T-shirts and dropped them, crumpled, onto the towels they had spread over the sand.

Nikki ran with them across the hot sand to the edge of the water, anxious to cool her burning soles. But when the first wave curled over her feet, she jumped back out of the icy water with a shriek.

"How can they do that?" Carly said, nodding her head at the twins, who were splashing and somersaulting in neck-deep water. "I don't think they have any feeling. . . . HEY!" Her voice lifted in a shout as Jeff grabbed her from behind. He high-stepped through the waves, struggling to hold on to Carly, who pushed and flailed at him with her fists.

"Put me down, you idiot!" Carly yelled at her brother. "Stop it! What are you, some Neanderthal? Put me *down!*"

But Jeff held on tight. When the water reached his waist, he tossed her in and turned back toward the beach, wiping away the water that had splashed his face. He beat on his chest with clenched fists as he ran, giving a great echoing Tarzan yell. He started toward Nikki, who turned and ran.

Trying to get away in the soft, burning sand was useless. Jeff was behind her in a second, grabbing her under the knees and arms. Nikki struggled wildly, just as Carly had, but he lifted her off the ground with little effort and started back toward the water.

"Will you just put me down? I don't want to do this, Jeff. Listen to me! I don't want—the water's freezing. . . ."

Jeff glanced down at her as he ran, laughing. Then he realized suddenly that she hadn't even taken off her T-shirt. Her eyes were dark blue, wide and panicked, as she stared back at him, pushing on his chest with both hands. He stopped abruptly and slid her gently upright to the sand in front of him.

She took a great breath of air. "I was afraid . . ." Her heart beat so fast she could barely speak. "I was afraid I . . . would throw up in . . . front of everybody." She caught her breath and turned on him. "Don't you have any brains at all?" Jeff reached out to steady her arm, but she yanked away. "I can't play around like that anymore."

"What a jerk," he said, his lips tight.

"Thanks a lot!"

"Not you—I mean me. I wasn't thinking, Nik. I got goofing off like we used to, and I forgot. I'm sorry." He put his arm around her shoulders, apologizing with his touch, but she shrugged him off.

"And don't start treating me like I'm made of glass either," she said. "I just want to be treated like everyone else, okay? Except you can't throw me around because I—"

Nikki jumped backward as a bucketful of lake water cascaded over Jeff's head, soaking his hair in dark, jagged strands to the tip of his nose and dripping off his chin. He gasped for air, blinking hard, and wiped a few slick, green strings of algae from his cheek.

Behind him, Carly grinned at the little girl in a yellow Minnie Mouse bathing suit who stood beside her, giggling. Carly handed her the now-empty red bucket.

"Thanks, sweetie. Us girls gotta stick together, right?"

The child giggled again, then ran off clutching her bucket.

"Wait'll I get my hands on you," Jeff sputtered as he tore down the beach after his sister.

Nikki sank back onto the rumpled towels, breathing in short, shallow breaths, trying not to move her midsection where the nausea roiled. She could see Adam and Abby from where she sat, but it was several minutes before Jeff and Carly returned. They were both dripping this time. Jeff held out a huge cup of Coke to Nikki, watching her eyes as she reached for it. She smiled her thanks, and he dropped down beside her.

Carly put her hands on her hips. "I suppose you need a rest after all that macho activity, right? Oh, well, I may as well go keep track of the twins, since I'm all soaked anyway, thanks to you." She ran back down the beach, her short, blond hair gleaming in the sun, her movements lithe and graceful.

"She's starting to look just like your mom," Nikki said as she watched Carly plunge into the water. She wondered how it would feel to be Carly. *Her parents think they're privileged to have her around. She never worries about coming up with the right thing to say to people. And she would never, ever let herself get into a mess like I have.* Nikki sighed.

"Yeah, she definitely came out ahead of the rest of us in the looks sweepstakes," Jeff said. "Listen, you said the other day that Coke helped your stomach, so I thought maybe this would . . ."

"It does. Thanks."

Jeff lay back on the towel, squinting against the bright sky. "Nik? I really am sorry."

She shook her head. "Just forget it, all right?" She took a long drink of icy cold soda, and they were silent for a moment. Then she spoke again. "Grandpa knows."

"About the *baby?*"

Nikki looked around uneasily. "Jeff, do you have to yell? Maybe I'd rather everybody on the beach didn't know."

He sat up straight. "How'd he find out? From your mother?"

Nikki shook her head and described the conversation with her grandfather. Then she added, "In a way, I'm kind of relieved that he and Gram know. I didn't think I could stand lying to everybody much longer. At least now I can talk to him about things—you know, ask him what he thinks."

"Well, yeah, if anybody would know what to do, I'd think it would be your grandpa. What'd he say?"

"He brought up something I hadn't even thought about— having the baby and giving it up for adoption."

"Nikki, that'd be great. I mean, that way you get to go on with your life, and the baby doesn't have to die. . . ."

"Oh, right! You make it sound so easy. Well, let me tell you, it's not. Sometimes, late at night when I can't sleep, I think about this baby, you know? And I—I care about it. I try not to, but I can't help it. So tell me, if adoption's such a great idea, how am I supposed to go through seven more months of this, plus labor and delivery, and then just hand the baby over to some stranger? Now, there's a terrific idea, sure. Terrific for everyone but *me*."

Jeff brushed the sand off the top of his feet, and the bones showed sharply through his tanned skin.

"You know, Nik, Dad works with an adoption agency back home. Some church runs it. If you ever want to talk to him, I know he'd be glad to help." He thought for a moment, then added, "I don't think anybody's stupid enough to say this is an easy option, not even me. But it just may end up being the best one you've got."

"I don't know what to think. I feel like I'm going nuts. How could I live with myself if I have an abortion? On the other hand, do you realize where that leaves me? I feel like I'm being backed into a corner, and no matter what I do, I can't get out."

Just then, the twins raced back to the towels, looking for something to drink. Nikki handed the rest of her Coke to Abby, who took a long drink, then blew bubbles through the straw.

"Aw, come on!" Adam cried. "Don't backwash in the Coke. I want some, too! Jeff, make her give me some."

Jeff and Nikki glanced at each other, silently acknowledging that their conversation was over.

Lights bobbed across the lake by the time Jeff finally turned *Another Line* back into the Rosendale channel. He cut the motor as they came out of a turn, and the boat glided almost silently past the "NO WAKE" sign.

On the pier, people strolled and fished, and some waved at the passing boats. Watching them, Nikki couldn't help remembering how she used to walk the pier nearly every summer night, sometimes with Gram and Grandpa, more often with Jeff and Carly.

Water lapped the sides of the channel with tiny splashes in the soft, summer darkness, and laughter carried over the swells from the pier. Nikki tried to lose herself in the beauty like she used to, but there was too much on her mind. *Well*, she thought, letting herself rock slightly with the motion of the boat, *if I can just make up my mind what to do, I can start to climb out of this hole. At least things can't get any worse.*

Nikki pushed open the screened door to the back porch and stumbled over the step in the darkness. The swing creaked, and she realized she was smelling cigarette smoke in the air.

"Dad? What are you doing here?"

Gram always made Nikki's father smoke on the porch, because she hated the smell in the house.

"Your mother called and asked me to come get her. Her play opens Thursday night, and my case is in recess until Tuesday, so here I am."

"When are you going back?"

"Not till tomorrow night. We have a little business to take care of here first."

Tomorrow night. Nikki caught her breath. Once they left, she would have her car back. She could go to the clinic whenever she wanted.

If she wanted.

Her father's last words reached her then.

"What business?" she asked.

"I would think you'd be able to figure that out."

"What are you talking about?"

"Sit down, Nikki."

She sat on the edge of the wicker rocking chair and clutched hard at the arms. Suddenly, she knew what was coming.

"Your mother tells me there's been another little development here besides your grandmother's stroke." There was silence for a moment. "Well?"

"Well what?"

He swore under his breath, and she could see the glowing end of his cigarette fade as he wedged the butt into the old saucer Gram gave him for an ashtray.

"People who play games anger me, Nikki. Your mother says you're pregnant, about two months gone."

It was no use. She couldn't pretend. "Yes."

"Well, that was a pretty stupid move. But at least it's easy to take care of at this stage."

"Take care of?"

A lighter flared for a second as he held it to the tip of a new cigarette. In its light, Nikki could make out his black, silky eyebrows over his shadowed eyes. Then the flame went out with a thin, metallic snap.

"Take care of, get rid of, however you want to dress it up."

"But . . . but suppose, maybe, that I don't want to do that?"

He gave a short laugh. "Your mother told me about your conversation. Listen, Nikki, there are other things on the line here. Important things, like—" He got to his feet, and she heard him move toward the kitchen doorway. "I don't want to discuss this right now. I only came out here for a cigarette. I've had a rotten day, to say nothing of finding out that my only daughter's gotten . . . Anyway, we'll have time to talk tomorrow. Plenty of time."

Nikki sat still in the rocker after he disappeared inside. She automatically started peeling at her fingernails but caught herself in time. She stuffed her hands in her pockets and sat, rocking, until she heard him go up the stairs.

Nikki tossed back and forth endlessly that night. Her bedroom was stiflingly hot. There was hardly any breeze from the lake. She kicked off the light summer blanket, then the sheet, and lay on the mattress in only her thin cotton shirt and panties.

In a little while, a light breeze kicked up, and she struggled in the dark to pull the sheet back over her. When the breeze stopped, she pushed the sheet aside impatiently. On, off. On, off. Soon the bed was a twisted tangle.

Like my mind, she thought, breathing heavily in the close, humid darkness. *I don't have a clue what to do. If I get the abortion, I'm killing another person. A baby. My baby.*

If I don't, it means seven months of this and I can't take it anymore. I wish someone would just make the decision for me—just tell me what to do. If I have an abortion, I'm killing another person. If I don't, I may as well die.

Her thoughts spiraled around an endless loop, fuzzy and indistinct on the brink of sleep. She dozed and woke, still thinking, then dozed once more. When the breeze woke her again, she wiped her wet face on the pillowcase and couldn't tell if the wetness was sweat or tears or both. She pushed herself up on one arm, flipped over the damp pillow, and flopped down again.

I'm losing my mind. She stared into the darkness over the bed. Then she prayed silently. *God, listen to me, if You're there. I need help. I don't know how to talk to You.*

She waited in the darkness. For what, she didn't know. There was only silence. And more darkness.

She remembered when she was small, watching Gram kneel by her bed at night, teaching her to say her prayers.

"Gram always said You are everywhere," she whispered into the darkness, "that You can hear everything we say, so if You can hear me now, please help. I don't know what to do. Please, please help me."

She tried to think of the Bible verses she had learned as a child when her grandparents took her to Sunday school, back when she'd believed the whole Christianity thing without question. All she could remember was "The Lord is my shepherd, I shall not want." *I'm not even sure what that means*, she thought.

Nikki searched her mind for anything else, but all she could come up with was the verse on Gram's needlepoint sign over the kitchen table: "Show me the way I should go, for to you I lift up my soul." *At least it makes more sense than the shepherd thing.* She said it over to herself several times. It didn't make her anxiety go away, but it broke the endless cycle of her thoughts enough that she could relax. Eventually she drifted back into sleep.

Fourteen

THERE WAS A SHARP KNOCK, and the bedroom door opened a crack.

"Nikki, it's eight o'clock. Get up and get dressed. We're going out to breakfast."

She lay still for a minute, her eyelids too heavy to open. Last night's confusion rushed back in on her—it was like waking up from a nightmare, only in reverse. And the minute she moved, there would be the morning sickness to contend with and the spasms of retching that went on and on. Breakfast with her parents was a good idea, though. Not that she wanted any food in her stomach, but maybe they could finally talk this out.

And I won't let them push me around either. This time I'll make the decision.

Downstairs, her parents were drinking coffee at the dining room table. Mr. Sheridan was smiling, as near to jovial as he ever got outside the office.

"We were just about to send out a search party, Nikki," he said.

"Sorry." She avoided his eyes.

"I'm only joking with you. Don't be so serious."

Nikki looked up at him from under her eyebrows. What was he up to, anyway?

Nikki's mother gathered up the coffee things. She wore her usual pained expression, the lines around her mouth etched more deeply than Nikki had noticed before. *She's getting old and she knows it*, Nikki thought suddenly. You couldn't tell from the model-slim body encased in her tight-fitting top and stretch pants, or from the perfectly manicured nails—but you could tell from the lack of light in her eyes and the frown lines on her forehead.

It was different with her father. His dark-brown hair was wavy and thick, and his olive complexion showed no wrinkles. There was no joy in his face either, but there was a kind of driving intensity. Even Nikki could see how female clients would be attracted to him. There was a charisma about him, but she knew it was only a thin veneer.

He pushed back his chair and got to his feet.

"Come on, let's get going. Rachel, are you ready?"

Picking up her bag, she replied, "Just waiting for you."

"Where's Grandpa?" Nikki asked. "Isn't he coming?"

"He left for the hospital long before you got up," Mrs. Sheridan answered. "He couldn't wait to see your grandmother."

Nikki felt a twinge of uneasiness. Suddenly, she wanted Grandpa there with them. "Where are we eating?"

"We thought we'd drive into Ardmore," Mr. Sheridan said.

"Ardmore? For breakfast? That's an hour away!"

"We'll get something on the way if you can't wait," her father answered. He locked the kitchen door behind them, and they walked to their car.

"This seems awfully far to go for breakfast," she protested again.

No one answered her.

"I mean, people don't usually drive an hour to get pancakes, you know?"

"Just get in the car, Nikki, and stop asking questions." Mr. Sheridan held open the back door for her, and Nikki could see a muscle twitch in his jaw. She hesitated a moment, but his stare unnerved her. She slid into the beige leather interior. It was hot from the morning sunshine, but her feet and hands felt icy.

"I told you last night we had some business to take care of." He turned the key, and the engine sprang to life.

"Business? Dad, what's going on?"

Her parents glanced at each other, and Mrs. Sheridan made an elaborate show of finding her lipstick and redrawing her mouth.

Nikki swallowed hard and tried again as they passed Rosie's Grill. "I want to know why we're going to Ardmore."

Looking at Nikki's reflection in the visor mirror, Mrs. Sheridan said, "Your father has a friend there, an old friend from college who's a doctor. We're taking you to see him."

"*What?* What kind of doctor?"

"An OB/GYN."

"Wait a minute. What do you mean? Why are—?"

"Look, Nikki," her father said, "he's agreed to see you as a favor to me, to take care of your . . . problem."

"But I—"

"He's in a large, well-staffed practice," Mr. Sheridan continued. "They have an excellent reputation in the area. He's very competent, and I'm sure—"

"Wait a minute!" Nikki broke in. She leaned forward over

the back of her father's seat, her fingers digging into the uphol-
stery. "What do you think you're doing? This is supposed to be
my decision. It's me who's pregnant, remember?"

"And you obviously have no idea what to do about it," he
answered. "So we're doing what parents are supposed to do—
we're helping you."

Nikki fell back against the seat, her eyes closed. "I can't
believe this. I can't believe you're ... Isn't this against the law or
something? What do you think this is, 1930?"

Her father slammed his open hand against the steering
wheel, and the big car jerked slightly to the right. He yanked
the wheel back.

"You're making a spectacle of yourself, David." Mrs.
Sheridan's voice was quiet, warning.

Nikki leaned forward again. "You can't make me do this if
I don't want to. You can't force me into it. Just because I haven't
got the answers all figured out yet doesn't give you any right to
push me into an abortion. You've never cared what I do. What
difference does it make to you now?"

"That's enough out of you, Nikki!" her father said. "You got
yourself into this situation through your own stupidity, and we're
doing our best to get you out of it. And all you give us is lip."

"But I don't understand!" she cried. "What business is it of
yours whether I have this baby or not?"

Mr. Sheridan snorted and started to answer, but Nikki's
mother stopped him with a small shake of her head. She half
turned in her seat to face Nikki, but her gaze slipped just a little
to the side.

"Lower your voice, Nicole," she said. "I have no intention
of being yelled at all the way to Ardmore. I explained this to
you the other day in the kitchen. Abortion is perfectly legal,

perfectly safe, and in your case it's the only option that makes any sense at all."

"Sense from whose viewpoint? How about *my* viewpoint? How about the *baby's?*"

"It's a fetus, Nicole, and stop raising your voice. Be reasonable. You're going back to school in just over a month. Do you really want to be pregnant when you walk through those doors? You can't hide it forever, you know. In fact, I think you're starting to show a little already."

Nikki looked down at her stomach quickly and yanked at her shirt to flatten it.

"Can you imagine how . . . what was his name, B.J.—?"

"T.J.!"

"Whatever. Can you imagine what he'll say when he sees you? Not to your face, of course. Behind your back. And that's the least of it. You want to go on to college. You're very talented in music, you're interested in psychology. Exactly where does a baby fit into those plans?"

Nikki sank back against the seat. Her mother's words brought back the hollow feeling in her chest, the dark emptiness she had been fighting all week. So far, she had almost avoided thinking about school, except for those few times late at night. But with just a few deft strokes, her mother had penciled in a clear picture of what she knew was coming. The guys would mock her unmercifully. And Lauren . . . Nikki could just see her and the other girls whispering in the locker room and in the hall between classes. Nikki could almost hear the hiss of the word *stupid* in her ears.

"Well?" her mother said.

Nikki shook her head, her eyes closed. How could she talk over all the noise in her head?

Mr. Sheridan finally had control of himself again. "You see,

Nikki, we may not always have come across to you as loving and caring as you would have liked, but we have your best interests, your welfare, in mind." His voice was composed and slick-sounding. Nikki had the distinct impression he was reading from a script. "We want to help you with this. They'll take very good care of you at Richard's office, no worry about that."

Nikki began to work at her thumbnail until she produced a small slit, then peeled it to the quick. She spread her hands on her lap and surveyed the other nine carefully manicured, polished nails. Methodically, one by one, she peeled them off and dropped the pink bits onto her father's immaculate beige carpet.

How can they get away with this? Why isn't there someone here who can help me? she cried inside. *What about You, God? Is this how You answer all those prayers I prayed last night? If You don't mind my saying so, this doesn't seem like much of an answer to me.*

And yet, Nikki was aware of another feeling growing within, right alongside the anger. It was a kind of relief. She could picture Grandpa's eyes when he found out. Jeff's, too. And she could already hear her own defense.

"Look, they made me do it," she would say. "I had no choice. What was I supposed to do? Jump out of the car going 70 miles an hour?"

All she had to do was stop fighting, let it happen. Who could blame her?

Nikki stared out the window at the flat Michigan countryside blurring by at well over the speed limit. She kept swallowing, trying to force down the tight, hard lump that threatened to choke her. What a relief it would be to throw herself down on the seat and howl, sob and kick and scream bloody murder, but she wouldn't give them that.

She made one last attempt. "I won't do it."

"You don't want to be reasonable?" her father thundered. "Fine. Then let me put it to you straight. There is no way you're coming back to Millbrook pregnant. Period. Do I make myself clear? ... Well?"

Like snapping a high-powered lens onto a camera, his words clicked everything instantly into focus. Nikki sat forward.

"Wait a minute."

How could she have been so blind?

"This isn't about me at all, is it? This is about *you*. You're afraid you won't get that judgeship if they find out I'm pregnant. They wouldn't want someone presiding over family court whose own daughter—"

"Shut up, Nicole!" he shouted. "You're going too far."

Her mother was talking over him, way too fast. "Don't be ridiculous, Nicole. You're all upset. You're just jumping to conclusions."

But Nikki knew. And knowing, she saw them with different eyes and felt a whole new kind of fear. Until now, she'd always assumed that, in their own strange way, they loved her and just didn't know how to show it. But now ... A little shiver of cold ran up her spine. Where his career was concerned, Mr. Sheridan never allowed anything to stand in his way.

When they arrived in Ardmore, Nikki saw that the doctor's office was just a normal-looking brown brick-and-smoked-glass building in a pleasant older neighborhood. Norway maples cast dense shadows on the sidewalk in front. Two little kids were riding Big Wheels in a driveway next to the parking lot, their plastic wheels rattling across the blacktop.

This can't really be happening, Nikki thought as they got out of the car. *Someone will see what's going on. Someone will stop it.*

But they made their way to the front desk unchallenged, Mr. Sheridan's hand guiding Nikki, his fingers pressing into the icy skin of her elbow.

"My daughter, Nicole Sheridan, has an appointment with Richard—that is, Dr. Steiner."

The receptionist's hands were full. In one she held a phone, which she was struggling to position between her shoulder and ear; in the other was a pen, and with it she scrawled words across a receipt form while a patient drummed her fingers in irritation on the counter.

The receptionist lifted a forefinger, signaling for Mr. Sheridan to wait, then flipped a white rectangle of paper onto the counter toward the impatient woman.

"Here's your receipt, ma'am. Sorry about the wait." She turned her attention to the phone. "Sorry to keep you waiting. . . . I know, but our computer's down and our office manager's gone home sick. . . . Yes, we can probably work you in about four o'clock, but you must understand there'll be a wait. . . . Can you hold?" Another phone line rang, then another. After several minutes, she glanced up at Mr. Sheridan and Nikki and produced a tight-lipped smile in their direction.

"I'm sorry. It's an absolute madhouse here today."

"No problem," Nikki's father said in his smooth-to-the-client voice. "How long do you think it'll be?"

"I'm not sure, sir. We're very short-handed. Just take a seat and fill this out, please." She held out a blank health history form to Nikki.

They sat down in the mauve upholstered chairs beside a tank full of exotic-looking yellow-and-black fish. Nikki folded her arms across her chest, letting the paper slide to the floor.

"I'm not doing this," she whispered at her mother, who had taken a seat on the other side of her daughter.

Mrs. Sheridan picked up the form without a word and began to fill in the blanks.

Nikki's mind whirled. If she was going to have an abortion, she'd decide that on her own, thank you, not be pushed into it this way. They were treating her like . . . like some appliance that needed repairs. Like dropping off a TV and saying, "Here, fix this."

Think, she urged herself. *Think!* She had to come up with a solution, and fast, but her mind kept turning over uselessly, like an engine in neutral.

Her eyes darted around the room. It was filled with women, most of them obviously pregnant, and a few young husbands. She counted four different nurses bustling back and forth, leading patients to a small side room. Through the open doorway, Nikki could see the patients step on a scale, where most of them made dismayed faces. Next they had their blood pressure taken, then returned to the waiting area again until the doctor was free.

One other girl looked about Nikki's age. When their eyes met, the girl smiled and Nikki, amazed at the force of habit, found herself smiling back automatically.

What would happen if she stood up and yelled to the whole room what her parents were doing? These women, chatting about gaining weight, leafing through magazines with glossy covers of beautiful, smiling babies—what would they say? Would they do anything?

And what did she want them to do? Nikki looked down at her hands and folded them one over the other without thinking, so her jagged nails were out of sight.

Then, as though her body had a mind of its own, she felt herself stand up and walk toward the door. Her father was beside her before she reached for the knob, but he didn't stop her. As she turned it, Nikki glanced back. Mrs. Sheridan sat reading calmly, watching from under lowered lids. *Never make a scene*, Nikki thought. The words her mother lived by.

Outside, Nikki walked rapidly to the edge of the parking lot. Her father was right there.

"Well, Nikki?"

"I don't want to do this. You can't make me. I've thought a lot about it in the last week, and I've talked to some other people and done some reading, and I don't think abortion—"

"Nicole. Look at me." His voice was low.

She hesitated, knowing his dark, furious eyes could reduce her resolve to nothing.

"I said look at me . . . *now!*"

She met his eyes.

"I've worked 15 years to win this appointment. I promise you I will not lose it over this." The skin around his mouth was white, his jaw so tight the bones worked visibly to produce each word.

Nikki felt a thrill of fear ripple through her. *Not now*, she thought. *Don't fold this time.* She opened her mouth to answer, but as she did, a nurse appeared in the doorway and peered out into the parking lot.

"Nicole Sheridan? Your mother said you were out here. Please come in. We're ready for you now."

Nikki looked from the nurse to her father. He stared into her eyes and, staring back at him, she felt 10 years slide off her. Her knees began to buckle. She struggled to gather her strength. No, she wouldn't back down, she couldn't.

"Would you please come right away?" the nurse said, unable to mask the irritation in her voice. "We're terribly busy this morning."

Mr. Sheridan reached out and took Nikki's elbow again, his eyes still staring into hers, and turned her toward the building.

The nurse watched them, puzzled.

Under her gaze, Nikki reacted to the pressure on her arm without objection. She walked through the waiting room numbly. And as Mr. Sheridan released her to follow the nurse, it hit her—she'd become just like her mother.

She had never realized before that she had been fearing it all her life, but she knew it now. Keep up appearances at all costs. The family motto. She wanted to scream out to everyone she passed, "They're making me kill this baby!" But she couldn't. She couldn't make a scene. And her parents knew it.

Nikki followed the nurse down the hall.

"I tell you, I've worked here three years," the nurse was saying, shaking her head, "and I've never seen it like this. They put everything on the computer to streamline things, then the computer goes down and we're absolutely helpless." She flipped through an armload of files for Nikki's chart and, as she did, the entire stack of folders slid sideways and slipped from her grasp. Papers sprawled across the short-pile, gray carpet, patient records mixing together as smoothly as a well-shuffled deck of cards.

The nurse stared, open-mouthed, at the jumble on the floor, then heaved a resigned sigh. "This is absolutely the last straw. I can't believe this is happening. It'll take me hours to sort them out." She glanced up at Nikki, and her voice turned professional again. "Well, let me get you settled first, then I'll worry about this mess."

She motioned Nikki into a bright side room. There was a bulky black machine in the corner. Nikki looked at it and felt her stomach lurch.

"Here, take off everything except your smile," the nurse said, relieved to launch back into her canned speech, "and put on this blue gown, open in front. You can lay the sheet over you till we get started."

Nikki waited until the door clicked shut to begin undressing. She removed her shirt and shorts slowly, reluctantly, and hung them on the wall hook, then looked at her lacy flowered underwear.

She reached up and took her clothes off the hook. Then she hung her underclothes up first and arranged the shirt and shorts over them so they wouldn't show. She slipped her arms into the stiff, papery blue gown and climbed onto the table. One of the ties had ripped off the gown, so she sat clutching the sides together over her breasts, waiting. The air conditioning switched on, and soon little goosebumps stood out along her arms and legs.

How could I have let this happen? How do I always let them make me do what they want?

It seemed so cheap, so ugly, that this baby would die just because she didn't have the nerve to make a scene. And now it was too late. There was no way out.

This room doesn't even have a window, she thought wildly.

"Oh, God." Nikki leaned her head back against the wall and hugged her knees to her chest. Tears spilled from her closed eyes, and she shook her head back and forth slowly. "Oh, God, why am I such a loser?"

There was a brisk rap at the door and a different nurse entered, a stocky, smiling woman with gray mixed through her cropped brown hair.

"All ready to see if we can zero in on this little guy? Or girl, as the case may be?"

Nikki looked down, pretending to blow her nose, and managed to get the tears off her face unnoticed. But inside, the nurse's words set off seismic shock waves. How could she be so nonchalant about this? Maybe when you helped with this many abortions they didn't faze you anymore. Maybe you stopped thinking about it being a person.

The nurse's thick hands were amazingly quick as she set things up. She keyed in a flurry of letters and numbers that printed out across the top of the monitor screen on the black machine. Then she turned to Nikki, pushed open her gown and pulled down the sheet that covered her.

"This'll be a little cold," she said and spread a large area of Nikki's abdomen with something that felt like liquid ice.

"What is that?" Nikki asked, startled at the chill of it.

"We call it belly jelly," the nurse answered with a smile. "There, I think you're all set. He'll be right in." She wiped her hands dry on a paper towel, tossed it in the trash, and left.

Nikki lay still, only her eyes searching the room. She wasn't sure what she had expected, but this wasn't it. Why the cold, sticky stuff on her stomach? Why the monitor? But then, what did she know? She'd never had an abortion. She'd never even been to this kind of doctor before.

She closed her eyes and saw again the tiny baby in the lighted cube at the museum, its miniature fingers and arms, its delicate legs and feet. She hadn't wanted this baby, no. But she hadn't meant for it to die like this either.

From the center of her being, a wave of sadness spread through her, followed by a wave of self-loathing. It was her fault. She should have found some way, any way, to stop it.

There was a click of the latch, and the door opened.

Fifteen

"HOW ARE YOU DOING?" The slight, red-haired man thrust his hand out to Nikki. Embarrassed, she barely shook it, then pulled her hand away. "I'm Tom Layton, and I'll be performing the procedure for you."

Tom Layton. That wasn't the name her parents mentioned. Besides, this guy was years too young to be a college friend of her father's.

"Where's the doctor?"

"Oh, you won't be seeing the doctor this visit. Why, were you expecting to?" But he didn't wait for an answer. Instead, he positioned himself on a stool midway between the bed and the monitor.

Nikki frowned. Something was definitely wrong here. She glanced at the screen. Words appeared in the upper left corner, words the nurse had typed off the patient records. She had to squint, but she could make them out.

Lisa M. Van Woorden. The name was followed by a phone number she didn't recognize. Nikki thought of the patient folders that had spilled in the hall, the records jumbled together.

The man swiveled his stool around so that he could face both Nikki and the screen, and he pressed a wand gently against her belly.

"Listen, I think . . ." she began.

"Hold on, hold on," he said, raising his free hand to stop her. "Almost got it. There. See?" He pointed to the screen, smiling.

At first Nikki couldn't make any sense of what she saw. The closest thing she could think of was the old NASA footage televised every July, the pictures of men landing on the moon. Lots of static, a strange blunt shape turning and twisting in a wedge of picture.

"See, there's his head," Tom pointed to the screen. "Or hers, of course. It's still too early to tell. Now watch—you'll see him move."

As though on cue, the tiny figure seemed to fold itself over, then stretch.

Nikki stared. It was magical, seeing what was going on inside her. With the technician's help, she could make out the little hands and the minuscule legs that ended in feet as small as those she'd seen in the museum. She forgot to explain that she was not Lisa M. whoever, that there had been some kind of mistake here. The whole ugly morning was sponged from her mind as she stared at the tiny being on the screen.

Kick, stretch. Kick, stretch. Straight up, to the right, roll completely over. Slow motion, underwater ballet. Nikki's throat began to ache, and she realized she was holding her breath. She took in air slowly, cautiously, not wanting to disturb the child. Kick, stretch.

Suddenly, without warning, a tickle started in Nikki's nose, and she sneezed before she could stop herself. The figure on the screen went into a flurry of kicks.

"See how she responds to you?" the technician laughed. "That probably felt like an earthquake to her."

"She . . . he . . . whatever it is . . . can feel what I'm doing?"

"Sure can. The amniotic fluid all around her acts as a cushion, of course, but that doesn't keep her from feeling movement. Later on in the pregnancy, she'll be able to hear your voice, too, through that fluid. When babies are born, they already know their mother's voice, because they've been hearing it for months."

He laughed. "You know, I think you've got a real acrobat here." There was another series of kicks and stretches on screen. "All right. Enough for the entertainment. You lie as still as you can now, and I'll get the measurements."

He stopped the screen, frame by frame, measured and typed. He moved the wand against her stomach, and the tiny child danced again. He stopped the screen once more and entered more numbers.

"I didn't know it could move like that," Nikki murmured. "I never felt anything."

"No, you wouldn't, because he's so tiny. You won't feel anything till you're four or five months along. People used to use the term *quickening*—that's the first time the mother feels the baby's movements. They used that as a sort of cut-off time for abortion. But we know now that quickening has a lot more to do with what the mother's able to feel than with what's really going on inside. Chances are, most babies have been dancing around like junior here for a couple of months before the mother feels so much as a twinge."

The delicate body on the screen dipped and twisted, then straightened once again. As she watched, it came to Nikki that the child moved for joy—the elemental joy of living, of being, of existing. Here was life, exultant, in pure form. The baby's movements, though responsive to hers, were initiated totally by this other person. Nikki could feel herself smiling, the child's joy becoming hers.

"Okay, I'm just about done," Tom said. "Let's get a look at that heart and then we'll finish this up." He waited a minute, until the baby was still, then pointed with his pen to a recurring flutter in the center of the miniature body. "See it? Looks good. Listen now. I'll turn on the Doppler, and you'll hear it."

Nikki watched the flicker that drummed out the message of the baby's existence, and then suddenly a fast, swishy thudding sound filled the room.

"Hear it? That's his heart beating."

A feeling stronger than anything Nikki had ever experienced swelled up inside her, engulfing her with a deep, strong love. She would help it live, she would give this child the time it needed to complete its promise.

She had thought she held the power of life and death for this being in her hands, that the choice was hers to make. She could see now it wasn't like that at all. She could no more kill this little person than she could kill Grandpa or Gram or Jeff.

She reached up and wiped tears off her cheeks. "Sorry," she said, though she wasn't really.

"Hey, women cry in here all the time," Tom said, waving her words away with one hand. "It's pretty emotional, the first time you see your baby. No need to apologize."

He hit the print button, and a flimsy gray-and-white paper curled out of the machine. He waited until the thin chattering of the printer stopped, then ripped the paper straight across and handed it to Nikki. "There you go." He smiled at her. "Baby's first picture."

Nikki took it in her hands and smoothed out the curled edges. It was a still-life of the joy on the screen.

Then she remembered. She ought to say something.

"Listen, before you go, there's something I . . ."

There was a beeping, then a loud page came over the intercom. "Tom Layton to room 10. Tom Layton, room 10."

"Sorry. Gotta run. It's nuts here today. Good luck." He was out the door.

Nikki sat on the edge of the table, staring at the paper in her hand. Eventually, she looked up, saw her clothes on the wall hook. Reluctantly, gently, she folded the picture, trying not to crease the edges hard, and hid it in the pocket of her shorts.

The magic of seeing the baby was still strong, and she dressed slowly, as though in a dream. She couldn't stop the joy that welled up inside her—joy just from seeing that new life, and from knowing, finally, what she had to do.

Her father saw her coming first. He nudged his wife and stood up from his chair. Nikki walked past him to the door.

When they reached the foyer, he spoke, and his voice had that oily slick tone to it again, that watch-me-do-the-loving-dad-routine sound.

"Sweetheart." He put his arm around her shoulders. "Are you okay? Did . . . everything go all right?"

Nikki stiffened her back so that his arm fell away and looked up to meet his eyes. "Everything went just fine."

She strode to the car and got in. Her parents followed, silent for once.

Nikki curled up on the backseat, one arm beneath her head, and closed her eyes. There, in the blackness behind her eyelids, a baby hung suspended on a screen—*her* baby. She wrapped her arms protectively around her stomach.

❧ *Sixteen* ❧

WHEN THEY PULLED INTO the driveway of her grand-parents' house, Jeff was just climbing into the Allens' red Bronco next door. He waved a hand in their direction, and Nikki slid across the car seat, opened the door, and started toward him.

"Nicole, I want you to come in and lie down for a while," her mother began, but Nikki didn't answer.

She walked across the strip of grass between the houses. Jeff saw her coming and met her there.

From the driveway, Mrs. Sheridan called again. "Nicole, I'd like you to come inside." Nikki kept walking. "Nicole!"

Jeff looked from Nikki to her mother, who stood beside the car with her hands on her hips, then back again. He fell in step beside her. "Hey, what's going on?"

"Just come with me, would you? I need to talk to you."

"Well, sure. I was just going down to Rosie's. You want to go there?"

"No, I don't want to be around other people."

The front door of the house slammed behind her parents.

Nikki sighed her relief when she heard it but kept up her pace toward the dune forest. She and Jeff made their way side by side to the crest of the dune. Finally, Nikki stopped, leaning back against the wooden railing.

She blew out a long breath through pursed lips, then started to talk. "You won't believe what they did this morning."

"Try me."

She gathered her thick, dark hair in both hands and held it up off the back of her neck for a minute, letting the air cool her skin.

"They took me to this doctor's office. He's a friend of theirs, up in Ardmore. They just called up and made an appointment for an abortion. They never asked me or talked to me about it or anything!"

"Oh, Nik, I can't believe they . . . " Jeff said, reaching for her hand.

She pulled her hand away and turned to grip the railing.

"Yeah, well, it didn't turn out exactly like they planned. I didn't even know what was going on, in the beginning. The nurse made me undress and lay down and everything, so I thought they were getting me ready for the abortion. Then this guy comes in and starts doing an ultrasound. Somehow, they got my chart mixed up with someone else's. I didn't know what to do."

She thought for a moment, then continued. "At first, I was just so angry at my parents I couldn't think straight, you know? Then I saw the baby on the screen, a kind of computer monitor. And I think that I finally did start to, well, think straight, if you know what I mean." Her voice grew softer, and her fingers, white-knuckled on the wood, loosened and relaxed. "Jeff, remember what you said, that day we talked up here, about giving another life a chance?"

He nodded.

"Well, it didn't make much sense to me then. I was too busy thinking about the baby as my problem, you know? But when I saw it—him, her, whatever—" she laughed suddenly, and turned to face him "—and he was stretching and kicking and moving around, I knew it was a . . . a whole other life. It's like I have no right to end it. It's not the baby's fault he's here. Does all this make any sense?"

He nodded at her, smiling.

"Jeff." Her eyes were bright with tears. "He was so beautiful, so perfect. And I got to hear his heart beating. When I saw him, I just wanted to . . . well, to take care of him."

She took a deep breath. "So now I don't know if I'm really angry or really happy or both at the same time. But either way, there's a big problem. Mother and Dad are going to find out there was a slight glitch in their plans, that I'm still pregnant. Then . . ." she crossed her arms in front of her and shook her head.

"Are you going to keep the baby?" Jeff asked.

"No. No, I can't do that. I told you Grandpa and I talked about adoption, and I thought about it all the way home this morning. I mean, there's no way I can give a baby any kind of decent life right now. But he said your father knows some adoption agencies in Chicago."

"Sure he does. Remember, I told you he's on the advisory board for one of them."

"Well, do you think he'd talk to me? Now? I kind of need to know right away, you know? Once my parents find out I'm still pregnant . . ."

Jeff straightened up and started down the steps. "Well, come on. He's not doing anything, just watching a game on TV."

Nikki started after him, then stopped. "Jeff? I just thought of something. If I got the ultrasound that was meant for some-one else, do you think—maybe—someone else got the abor-tion I was supposed to have?" She thought of the girl who had smiled at her in the doctor's waiting room.

"No way. They would've made her sign all kinds of papers first, and she'd have known something was wrong. The worst that could've happened was some nurse got reamed out for mix-ing up the charts." He turned and started back down the steps.

Dr. Allen, dressed in white shorts and a Chicago Cubs T-shirt, was sprawled barefoot on the couch, a newspaper over his face. Jeff pointed the remote at the screen, and the TV went black.

"Hey," a muffled voice came from under the paper. "Turn that back on. How's a guy supposed to get any rest around here?"

"Dad, get up, would you? Nikki needs help."

Dr. Allen yanked the paper off his face and sprang to his feet. "What's wrong?" he asked, suddenly all business.

Marlene Allen came out of the kitchen, her hands full of folded towels. She looked from one face to the other. "What's wrong?" she echoed.

"It's not an emergency or anything," Nikki said, her cheeks flushed. "Well, I guess it is, kind of."

Between Nikki and Jeff, they explained the situation quickly.

"They won't let me go back home pregnant, but there's no way I'm having an abortion now, not after what I saw this morn-ing," Nikki concluded. "So I need to get all the information from you about adoption and see if I can figure out, you know, what to do next."

Mrs. Allen dumped the towels on the rocker. She reached out and put gentle arms around Nikki, pulling her close. "Oh,

Nikki, what a terrible time for you. But what a fine decision you've made."

With his hands jammed into the pockets of his shorts, Dr. Allen paced to the broad picture window, then back across the polished wood floor to stand in front of Nikki.

"Nikki, do you understand this will be one of the most difficult things you ever do? In your entire life?"

"I . . . I think so."

"And one of the most worthwhile?" he added.

She nodded, returning his smile.

"Nikki, it's terribly painful to give up a child you've borne. You will love that child, think about that child, *wonder* about it, the rest of your life. Do you understand that?"

She swallowed hard and tears filled her eyes. "I'm not changing my mind."

He stared at her for a long minute, and Nikki had the feeling she was being measured. Then his smile broke out again.

"You're quite a girl, Nikki, quite a girl." Then, in an instant, he was all business again. "I think the first thing we have to do is talk to your grandpa, which means we'll all need to go in to the hospital. Where's Carly and the twins?" he asked his wife.

"I asked her to keep an eye on them down at the beach this afternoon."

"Good," Dr. Allen said. "Let's just leave her a note and get going."

"She's not gonna be happy about being left out of this," Jeff put in.

"Well, we don't have the time to do anything else. I'll just have to explain it to her later—with Nikki's permission, of course." Turning to his wife, he said, "How soon can you be ready, honey?"

"Just give me five minutes, okay?" Mrs. Allen answered, already heading up the stairs.

"Why the big hurry, Dad?" Jeff asked.

"I think we need to let Roger know what happened this morning and get his input. Nikki has several decisions to make, and it'll help if we have everything in place before Rachel and David find out what really went on at that doctor's office."

It meant another long ride for Nikki, but this time she felt protected and safe. Jeff's parents talked with her about adoption most of the way to the hospital, pointing out the possible problems and answering every question she could think to ask. By the time they stepped off the elevator on the fourth floor at the hospital, Nikki felt more confident than ever that her decision was the right one.

Grandpa looked up, surprised to see them in the doorway, and stood to greet them. "I didn't know you all were coming in today. Look who's here, Carole." He looked closely at their faces and stopped. "Is everything all right? Nikki, are you okay?"

Gram was sitting in the big turquoise chair by the head of the bed, her hair freshly washed and styled, a cane leaning on the bed nearby. Her smile included them all, and though the left side of her mouth still sagged, the smile was as sweet as ever. Nikki crossed the room to hug and kiss her.

"Hi, Gram. You look beautiful, you really do," Nikki whispered.

Gram's eyes smiled back at her, but when she opened her mouth to speak, no words came. She was still locked in silence.

"Rog, Carole, we need to talk," Carl Allen said.

Jeff got himself an extra chair from the lounge across the

hall, and Dr. and Mrs. Allen sat side by side on the bed. Once everyone was settled, Nikki explained again what had happened that morning.

Grandpa's jaw worked as she talked, his lips compressed into a tight line. Nikki had just finished describing the baby's movements on the ultrasound screen when there was a sound at the door. She stopped and looked up to see her parents standing there.

"So that's what really happened!" her father said. "No wonder you felt well enough to run off with Jeff as soon as we got home. I think the least you could have done was to tell us the truth instead of lying to us."

"I didn't lie to you. I—"

"Wait a minute," Grandpa said, rising from his chair, red patches high on both cheeks. "The real question here is, how could you possibly have tried to force Nikki into having an abortion that way? Your own daughter. Don't you know what that could have done to her?"

"It was for her own good," Nikki's mother replied, glancing at her daughter with narrowed eyes. "It's the only way out of this situation, without the rest of her life being ruined. I won't have her giving up every interest, every chance to make something of herself, for the product of some backseat encounter."

"Rachel, it's a life, it's a person," Grandpa said. "I've already talked with Nikki about adoption. This child deserves a chance to live, just like you, just like me. And it could be the answer to some couple's prayers."

"And what will Nikki do this year, while she's answering somebody's prayers? Go to school as though nothing's happened? Have the kids laugh and make fun of her, point fingers at her, have everyone in town know. . . ."

"Why don't you tell him the real reason you wanted the abortion, Mother?" Nikki stepped forward and stood beside her grandfather, facing her parents. "It has nothing to do with what's good for me. Or maybe you should explain it, Dad. Tell Grandpa how you might not get to be judge of family court if they find out how your own daughter screwed up. Tell him the only thing you can think of is how to erase what I did, any way you can, even if it means wiping out another life. Well, I saw this baby—my baby—today. That's not how you meant it to happen at the clinic, but it did, and there's no way I'm killing this child."

"Nikki, stop talking nonsense," her father said, his dark brows a straight, heavy line across his face. "You're 16 years old, and I'm telling you again, you are not coming home pregnant! You're right. I've worked years for a chance at being judge, and with the narrow-minded people back in Millbrook, your pregnancy would cost me everything I've worked for. And I won't pretend to be so high-minded as your mother—it's not just you I'm worried about, it's me. Me, understand? I went back to that lousy little town years ago to help out my father with his law practice when he got ill. And after he died, you were born, and we needed the money, and I've been stuck there ever since. So now it's my turn, you hear? My turn to at least make some kind of name for myself, to do something I want to do for a change." He broke off and fished in his shirt pocket for a cigarette.

From somewhere deep inside her, some part she'd never even known existed, Nikki found the strength to stand her ground. Having Grandpa and the Allens on her side was a big part of it. For the first time in her life, she sensed the strength that could come from a family. She turned to her mother.

"What about you? You and Dad don't even like each other.

Why'd you go along with him on this? What does his being a judge mean to you?"

Rachel Sheridan stared at her for a minute, then dropped her eyes. The room was silent.

Nikki's father gave a harsh laugh. "I'll tell you what it means to her. It means having a name in the community, maybe in the state. You'd be surprised how that advances a career, even a music career."

"And because of that, you'd force me to—"

"Oh, keep it, Nikki," her father interrupted. "I'm not going through all this again. Look, either have the abortion, or don't come home, understand?"

Grandpa moved forward slightly, his face furious, when suddenly, from behind them, began the most horrible sound Nikki had ever heard. Not a wail, not a grunt, but a painful cross between the two. Everyone in the room swung around to face the corner where Gram sat.

Her whole body was shaking with effort, and tiny beads of sweat stood out across her forehead. "MMMaaaaaaa . . . MMMMaaaaaaayyyyy hou . . ."

Grandpa was on his knees beside her chair in an instant. "Carole, what is it? What's wrong?"

She flung one arm out in frustration, and the cane clattered against the bedside table. "MMMyyy housss . . ." Her eyes burned at her daughter and son-in-law.

Suddenly, Grandpa sat back on his heels. "'My house.' That's what she's saying. If Nikki can't go home to Ohio pregnant, then she'll stay at our house, right, Carole? That's exactly what I was thinking."

Gram dropped her head in relief and sank back against the seat cushions.

Nikki stepped across the Allens' feet and knelt in front of her grandmother's chair. Tears streamed down her face. "You talked, Gram. You talked."

Gram shook her head, disgusted.

"No, listen, Gram. You can't quit! Maybe it didn't sound like much to you, but it's the beginning of really getting better. I know you can do it." She laid her head in Gram's lap and the bent fingers came to rest on her hair.

On the other side of the chair, Grandpa was crying openly as he watched his wife. "She's right, Carole. It's only a beginning, but for my money, that was the prettiest sound I've ever heard. Nikki," he turned to her, his face close to hers. "Would you like to stay with us? It won't be easy, honey, with your grandma's condition. She'll need a lot of help when she comes home. . . ."

"That's okay, Grandpa."

"You're doing the right thing, but it's not going to be easy. We'll do everything we can to get you through this."

Gram held one hand, and Grandpa took the other. From behind her, Dr. and Mrs. Allen spoke at once.

"And so will we . . ."

"We will, too . . ."

They stopped talking and smiled at each other. Mrs. Allen tried again. "We're only three hours away. You could come and spend some weekends with Carly, and we could work on setting up the adoption."

Dr. Allen nodded. "There are some wonderful couples on the waiting list. Some of them have been waiting years for a baby."

"Well, isn't this just great?" Mr. Sheridan said. "I'm glad you've got the situation all worked out to your satisfaction. It leaves us in a mess, of course. Don't you think people back in

Ohio will wonder what happened to our daughter? But what does that matter to you?"

Everyone turned and looked at him. He stood rigid with anger for a minute, then swiveled on his heel and stalked out of the room.

Mrs. Sheridan was left in the doorway, alone. She crossed slowly to Nikki, who stood up to face her. "Nicole, I'm sorry. Maybe I shouldn't have gone along with him on this. I hope . . . I hope someday I can make you understand why—" Her voice broke, the beautiful soprano voice Nikki had been hearing all her life, and she stopped. Then she reached up and lightly, ever so lightly, brushed Nikki's cheek with the back of her hand. She leaned over and kissed Gram, who made no effort to smile. Then she was gone, following her husband out the door.

Nikki stood rooted to the ground, and the others were silent, giving her the space she needed. *I finally stand up to them and everything falls apart. They're just walking out on me, leaving me.* For a minute, she thought the emptiness would swallow her whole.

Then Jeff caught her eye from where he sat by the door. His look was steady. Nikki felt strength come from him. And from his parents, who sat hand in hand on the bed, watching her.

She turned back to Gram and Grandpa, and there was goodness in their faces, and love. So this was what having a real family was like, she thought. A family that would be there when she really needed them. The kind of family she would find for her baby, no matter what it took.

Epilogue

November 18

Dear Jeff,

Thanks for the letter. I'm looking forward to Thanksgiving, too. I think it'll be really good for Gram to get out of the house. She's a lot stronger now, so the doctor here didn't have any problem with us coming to Chicago.

When she first came home in August, I never would've dreamed how much progress she'd make in three months. She can say a lot of words again, but it's still a struggle. Grandpa and I have to handle the cleaning and cooking because her left side is so weak. And she gets tired really fast. (Even if she didn't, I still don't think Grandpa would let her do anything heavy. He treats her like she's made of glass!)

School's okay. It's not like I'm really part of the class, though. I basically just go in the mornings, then I help out around here in the afternoons. It's not exactly what I had in mind for my junior year, you know? But it's not as bad as I thought either—

there's another girl in class who's pregnant, too. And at least I'll graduate on time next year.

Your parents were a real help when I was down there last weekend. I'm sorry you were gone, but I hear you guys won the tournament. Congratulations! Your dad and I spent Saturday morning with the social worker at the adoption agency, and we looked through files of about 15 families waiting for babies. I narrowed it down to eight, so far. It just seems like such a big decision...

Life changes really fast, doesn't it? I sure never dreamed I'd be spending my junior year picking a family for my baby.

You were a big help last summer, Jeff. I don't know which way I would've gone without some of the things you said to me up on the dune. To tell you the truth, I've had some pretty tough moments, wondering if I made the right choice. Then the baby moves around and I think, *Yes, this is what I have to do.*

Thanks for everything. I want to hear all about the basketball team (what I haven't already heard from Carly and the twins!). See you next week.

Love ya,
Nikki

P.S. Do me a favor—no wisecracks when you see me, okay? Maternity clothes aren't exactly my idea of high fashion.

If you or someone you know is considering abortion, or if you're seeking support or counseling after an abortion, you can find help under "Abortion Alternatives" in your local Yellow Pages, or you can contact Focus on the Family's Crisis Pregnancy Ministry, Colorado Springs, CO 80995; (719) 531-3427.